THE HAUNTING OF JAMAL JACKSON

THE LEFT HAND DUOLOGY:BOOK I

NAKIA COOK

VEILED THREATS PUBLICATIONS

THE HAUNTING OF JAMAL JACKSON

THE LEFT HAND DUOLOGY: BOOK I

The Haunting of Jamal Jackson: A Left Hand Duology: Book 1

Special Edition Hardcover by coversincolor.com

First edition October 2023

Veiled Threats Publications

ISBN 978-1-7774039-9-7 (e-book)

ISBN 978-1-7381315-0-1 (paperback)

ISBN 978-1-7774039-5-9 (hardcover)

To LEONARD COOK, one of my kindest fans. Thank you for all of your love and support, Daddy. It means a lot to me that you're able to see me out here doing my thing. Tell Lil' Bit we said hello and to behave.

ALSO BY
NAKIA COOK

Inamorata: A Rosewood Hollow Novel

Salarius: An Inamorata Novella, Book 2

Drummer Boy: A Short Story

The Deed: A Left Hand Duology Prequel Novella (paperback)

PROLOGUE

SHE RAN up the porch stairs, dropped the figurine into the mailbox, then ran to the biggest willow tree in the front yard.

"See you soon," she said, kissing it.

CHAPTER ONE

JAMAL JACKSON HAMMERED his custom realtor's sign into the lush lawn while his mind ran through a long to-do list. Open house was in a week. With a final tap, he drove the post deep into the thick grass and admired his chiseled medium brown face and gleaming white smile staring back at him from the sign. Everything had fallen into place without a hitch. It would be a total fuck up on his part if Thirty-five Spiegel Road didn't sell.

The heat and humidity were higher than normal this spring. He couldn't wait to get inside, turn on the air conditioning, and peel his sweaty shirt off his back. His eyes darted to the front door with longing, but relief from the heat would have to wait; he needed supplies from his Escalade. Although his vehicle sat parked in the driveway, it seemed miles away in the oppressive heat. He sighed and gathered his tools.

Three other agents had failed in selling this property, and Jamal knew why. Destiny. This was *his* house. If he couldn't sell it, no one could. He looked forward to snagging the commission check, but the bragging rights would feel as sweet as the money. He loved every minute of his career and rubbing it in the faces of his idiot colleagues was a bonus.

Jamal's calling was selling hard to move properties. He

couldn't explain it. Certain homes sent tingles through him. Coupled with whatever cosmic thing happened in the heavens, he was unstoppable. Today, his body buzzed with electricity. Something special was happening, and he was going to knock it out of the ballpark.

He looked forward to tucking away a big check. His wife, Qaylah, looked forward to spending it. She might get a little of the money, but no way was he letting her get her hands on most of it. That cash was meant for their savings account. Someday soon, they'd buy a dream house of their own instead of renting in the less than desirable neighborhood they lived in now.

"I'm excited for us, babe. We can pick out a color scheme for the nursery, and start choosing furniture," she had said during breakfast as she rubbed the imaginary swell of her belly.

"Qaylah, you're two months pregnant. Why are you rubbing your stomach? You didn't even realize you'd missed your period until I pointed it out," he said.

"I just feel so alive this time. I'm married to a wonderful man who's been a doting father figure to my daughter, and there's genuine love between you two. I've never been happier. This pregnancy is special for all of us, Jamal. Even Katie's excited to meet her new brother or sister."

Katie nodded at him with a mouth full of Cheerios. She didn't know her biological dad, Brian, well. Jamal was alright with that. He prided himself on being a worthy replacement.

When the time came, and Brian, who didn't care one bit for his three-year-old, popped up to ask Qaylah for money, or whatever drug addicts do when they resurface, Jamal would lay down the law. The impression he got from Qaylah was that Brian was belly up in a gutter somewhere, nearing the end of his heroin stash. When he returned, Qaylah wouldn't be alone.

This time, she'd have Jamal waiting by her side with a baseball bat.

"He shows up every six to eight months," Qaylah had said.

"Does he know you're Muslim now?"

"No, and I'm sure it will be a problem for him. He can't stay clean for more than a few hours, but he'll thumb his nose at us because we pray," she said, staring into the distance. "I can't believe that my mom and dad took his side and kicked me out of the family for converting."

"Religion is a scary thing for some people," Jamal said, his mouth full of toast. Unlike Qaylah's family, his parents and siblings leaned towards the fervent end of devotion. Jamal grew up loathing how much time they spent at the masjid.

His parents had converted before Jamal was born, breaking away from the Nation of Islam. They said they wanted to merge with the mainstream Muslim population. As civil rights activists, they proclaimed it their duty to project a positive image of Black American culture within the Sunni community.

"Son, solidarity is important. You can't isolate yourself from the rest of the Muslim world at large. You owe it to them and yourself to put your best foot forward, and show the world what an asset you are," his father had said.

Jamal found their pro-Black sentiments tiring. He'd been to one too many protests, and decided he was no one's Black Muslim role model. He was an ordinary guy who wanted to do great things.

He committed the better part of his twenties to their agenda. By the time his twenty-ninth birthday rolled around last year, he gave up and focused on his career instead of venturing too far into politics. His parents were supportive when he wanted to settle down and get married. The shock when they learned she was a white woman was priceless.

"I know we're all equal in the eyes of Allah," his mother began, "but couldn't you find a Black woman to bring home? There are so many beautiful young ladies from Senegal and Nigeria who would love to marry my beautiful baby boy."

"Isn't this what you wanted? Equal footing in the Muslim world?" he asked.

"This makes me nervous, Jamal. What will we talk about?"

"You'll talk about all the important stuff like you would with a Black woman, Mama."

"Right. Important stuff like what?" she asked, wringing her kitchen towel between her thick hands. She meant well but hadn't a clue how to put into practice what she had preached.

"You'll talk about me, of course."

"What?" His mother wound up her towel and popped him on the behind for that one. Mama had nothing to worry about. The entire family loved his wife from the start. Qaylah latched on to them, eager for a familial replacement, and they treated her like one of their own. The Jacksons took her to the masjid daily and taught her the ins and outs of her new religion. Qaylah's enthusiasm was appreciated. But Jamal was not inclined to join them.

He worked long hours, so hanging out at the masjid wasn't reasonable for him when there were tons of properties to sell. Real estate in Rosewood Hollow, Virginia was booming. People moved to the city from neighboring areas like Calliope Falls and Piedmont County in droves, and Jamal's planner filled to the brim with empty nesters from Richmond and D.C. who wanted cheaper properties with mountain views, like this house.

Spiegel Road was located in the trendy neighborhood of Ashbury Heights. According to the last three agents, no one wanted it. The bank foreclosed on the property eight months ago in an abrupt sale, and not one buyer submitted an offer.

Jamal hadn't bothered to find out who the previous owner was. *It makes no difference as long as I get my money.*

He reached into the back of his trunk and pulled out a bucket of cleaning supplies along with a mop and broom. In his hasty retreat to the house, he nearly missed the shadow standing next to him.

"Whoa, what are you doing?" Jamal stopped mid-air with his right foot hovering over a little black dog. "I almost stepped on you, buddy. Go on back to where you came from before somebody misses you."

The dog cocked its ear, then walked around and pissed on the back left tire. "What the hell are you doing, you little—"

"Hey, have you seen my dog?" A scruffy, tired-looking white man with a face and neck full of stubble traipsed through the grass in his bathrobe and slippers.

"Is that him?" Jamal said, pointing at the little beast as he finished marking the other tires. "I just got my new rims, man. He's messing up my ride."

"What's with you Blacks and cars? You're the same way with shoes, willing to kill over it if it isn't in pristine condition," the man said, spitting on the sidewalk near Jamal's cognac penny loafers. "He's just a dog. He doesn't know how precious your ride is, homeboy."

"You're right, dude. It's not the dog's fault that you trained him poorly," Jamal said, mopping his forehead with a handkerchief. The dog walked over to Jamal and sat down.

"You ought to cut down those willow trees. Burn 'em, maybe."

"I've got the landscaping under control, pops." The old man was off his rocker if he thought Jamal was going to destroy the house's best feature.

The man scowled at him. "Keep away from my dog, or else," the man said.

"With pleasure. Keep him away from this property and we'll have no problems." Jamal slammed the trunk and walked to the front porch, cleaning supplies and his buffalo leather satchel in tow. He put them down next to the door and unlocked it with a set of master keys.

Jamal dug out the fliers and overdue notices that stuffed the rectangular mailbox to the max and tossed it inside the house on a small side table in the foyer. The sound of a solid object hitting the bottom of the mailbox caught his attention. He fished around for it, and his hand landed on a hard tiny object. He swiped it out and looked at it.

"I don't know what you are, but you sure are ugly," Jamal said, looking over the clay figurine in his hand. It looked like some type of horned deer head on a plump woman's body. The eyes were painted black, but the rest of it was plain terracotta. He chucked it into his pocket, then picked up the cleaning supplies and crossed the threshold into the house.

The shock of cold air he needed to wake him up from his heat-induced stupor wasn't there. "My God," he said, dropping the supplies on the floor and rushing to the thermostat. He was gonna lose his shit if it was busted.

He tapped on the gauge, which sat on the coldest setting. Sliding the dial from one side to the other, he listened for the familiar whirring of an air conditioning unit coming to life. "Come on, not today." Jamal pinched the bridge of his nose and took a deep breath. He returned to the foyer and checked out the vent at the front door. No air.

"Shit. This is all I need," he said, reaching into his bag for a matching leather planner. It took a half an hour to negotiate a price for a serviceman to check out the AC within his time restraints. In the meantime, he didn't see how he was going to get much done in the stifling heat.

A walk-through cheered him up a little. There were no pests on the main floors or in the attic. That was a good sign.

Jamal pulled the cord attached to a lightbulb in the basement. "Damn." Down there, it was another story. The new owners deserved a clean slate, not the floor-to-ceiling boxes of trash he saw. Jamal hated leaving stale memories in a house.

He sneezed from the dust, but as far as his nose could tell, there wasn't the stink of mold or mildew anywhere. The hot water heater and furnace were brand new, and so were the washer and dryer. He'd get someone to come and cart out the boxes over the next couple of days.

His cellphone buzzed in his pocket. Qaylah had texted him. *It's time to pray - Love you, Qaylah.*

Qaylah was one of those people who had to pray as soon as the time came in or she'd have an aneurism. He shoved the phone back in his pocket. He'd pray later.

The sound of something banging outside the bank head doors drew his attention. *What the hell was that?* Maybe the air conditioning had kicked in after all.

Jamal reached up and turned out the light, then remembered the clay figurine in his pocket. It slipped from his grasp and landed on the floor. "Damn," he said, turning on the light again. He bent down between a section of boxes to pick it up but snatched his hand back as a shard cut a gash in his forefinger.

"Stupid junk," he said, taking care to pick it up from the other end. He tossed it into a box, then turned off the light and ran up the stairs. The house felt colder than it had before Jamal went down to the basement. Freezing. The AC was definitely busted.

He shivered as water from the kitchen tap encouraged the blood to pull back into his veins long enough to wrap his finger

9

in a wad of paper towel. It had gotten cold enough that he considered opening the windows to warm up the place.

He turned off the tap and studied the wound. A fair amount of blood streamed from it. Jamal recalled Qaylah nagging him about getting a first aid kit for the glove box. Had he purchased one? He couldn't remember. There had been more important things to worry about than Band-Aids. The blood wasn't letting up. All he could do as he strode to the front door was hope he'd gotten one.

Jamal yanked open the door with his good hand and fell back into the foyer, flat on his back, his head cracking on the slate tiles hard enough to make his teeth chatter. The sound of persistent banging hadn't come from the air conditioner, but from the pair of withered black feet dangling from the body swinging from the bent trunk of a willow tree. He watched in horror as the feet slammed into the bulkhead doors.

Unassisted by force, it swung faster. Jamal's eyes traveled up the length of the tattered turquoise dress, skirted over the broken and bruised neck to the bulging eyes and back to the feet.

Although they slapped and moved freely, the rest of the body moved in a stiff and disjointed manner, arms held tightly at the sides, long braids glued to the back and shoulders as if the mass were frozen solid above the ankles.

The pounding in and outside his head had become unbearable. Jamal covered his ears with his hands, even jamming his fingers deep into his ear canals to no avail. Creaking rope, banging feet, the reverb of the bulkhead door; the noises increased in decibels until he grew nauseous, wishing that he'd pass out.

He slammed the door, then crawled several feet into the house. Jamal couldn't say how long he'd sat there waiting for the noise to cease, but when the world fell silent around him, he felt an immense release of pressure.

Jamal stared at the front door, unsure of what awaited him in the front yard. Questions flooded his mind. Who was the woman swinging from the tree, and how had she gotten there? Didn't anyone else in the neighborhood hear the racket? He sat stupefied, unsure if he should assist the woman or stay where he was. It was some time before he worked up the nerve to open the door. He moved towards it, stretching his hand towards the knob. He started turning it.

Jamal's phone buzzed in his shirt pocket, rousing him. He opened his eyes and found himself lying on the floor in the kitchen next to a small pool of blood with the tap running. The wound was worse than he'd initially believed.

He got up from the floor, grateful that the bleeding had lessened. A fresh wad of paper towels replaced the old ones wrapped around his finger, and another one scrubbed the blood off the kitchen floor. He'd had one hell of a fever dream or whatever had happened to him while he lay passed out on the floor. Thinking about it left him trembling all over.

The reminder on his phone buzzed again. His boss, Saalih Ashraf, was making an announcement. He had twenty minutes to get to the other side of town for the agency's afternoon meeting. Jamal checked his reflection in a mirror hanging in the living room. He didn't look ready to take on a meeting at the office, but skipping out would look bad since everyone else would attend.

There was enough time to grab some juice to replenish his fluids, and pull himself together. He'd come back and finish cleaning later. By then, the feeling that something more sinister and substantial than a cut on the finger had happened to him should have subsided.

CHAPTER TWO

"DON'T you think it needs medical attention?" Hannah Jefferson, the receptionist, peered through her glasses at the nasty purple cut on Jamal's finger. It throbbed and hurt a lot more than it did earlier. He'd bled through his tiny pack of bandages that were in the glovebox, sans first aid kit.

"No, I don't think seeing a doctor is necessary. It's bleeding, but the wound is closing. I would like a couple of bandages, if you don't mind, Hannah."

"Here," she said, pulling a first aid kit out from her desk. "There's an ointment in there. Use that first." She gave him a handful of bandages and answered the phone.

"Thanks, Hannah," he said, wrapping the desk with his knuckles. He put on one of the bandages she'd given him and glanced at the empty boardroom; the meeting started in five minutes. He'd rushed for no reason.

Jamal ducked into the room and put his satchel and the extra bandages on the massive oak table at his usual seat, then stood in the corner. He made it halfway through his prayer before the voices of Chauncey Ellison, and his sidekick Renee Stillwater, disrupted his train of thought.

Jamal moved his lips, concentrating on every syllable. The

tactic usually worked, but not today. Their voices hushed as they noticed him in the room, but they kept on dishing secrets.

"They were getting it on in the break room," Renee said. Her voice grated his nerves. She'd spread rumors about her own mother if Chauncey would listen.

"Stop lying," Chauncey said. Jamal hated him, too, but for different reasons. Chauncey was his biggest competition. He arrived at the office at six in the morning. By early afternoon, Chauncey bragged about sales to anyone who would listen, usually that someone was Renee. He was a top contender for the corner office at the other end of the building, opposite a view of the cascading waters of the neighboring city, Calliope Falls.

The others weren't pulling in enough sales to dream of getting a better view than the gravel pit next to the new subdivisions popping up on this side of town. Jamal could at least look out of his window and see the comings and goings at a nearby banquet hall, but he wanted that corner office. If for no other reason than to piss off Chauncey and Renee.

Jamal squeezed his eyes shut. He couldn't think while they gossiped. And his finger hurt like hell. Each time he bowed and touched the floor, it sent sharp explosions through it. He gritted his teeth and rushed.

"Take your seats, everyone," Shannon, the admin in charge of the minutes, said. "Mister Ashraf is on his way; he's stuck in traffic."

"I wouldn't mind being stuck in traffic if I had a Jag," Tim Shan blurted out as he entered the room.

"Maybe you can ride in mine sometime," Chauncey said.

"Since when do you own a Jag, Chauncey?" Brooke White asked. She hated Chauncey too, but for different reasons. Brooke still burned with shame from the time she asked him out and he turned her down. In an office-wide email. Ashraf didn't like it, but Chauncey was one of his best sellers. What could he say?

"Since yesterday. I'm picking her up next week, and I can't wait to stare at her from my corner office overlooking the falls," Chauncey said. Most of the room congratulated him.

"As if," Jamal said, under his breath.

"You sound a little jealous, Jamal," Renee said.

"I don't care what he's driving," Jamal said. "I think it's funny that he thinks he's getting the corner office."

"I like healthy competition." Heads turned towards the doorway. Saalih Ashraf, owner of Ashraf Realty, walked in and closed the door.

Everyone put away their phones and gave the boss their undivided attention.

"You're right to feel hungry for that office, Jamal. You've been closing like mad," he continued. "And you, Chauncey, you're a shining star and have been since day one. There are a couple of others of you who are contenders as well. Renee. Tim. You should hound Chauncey, like Jamal is."

Jamal sat up in his chair a little straighter when the boss mentioned his success. Saalih Ashraf was a pillar among the elders in the Muslim community. Despite worshipping in different mosques, Ashraf's name was as familiar to Jamal as anyone else at his place of worship.

Jamal wanted to be just like him. A pious man who could afford a Jaguar and a big house with a gorgeous wife. He got a real estate license because of him and never looked back.

"As for the rest of you, try to shadow these people if you can," Ashraf said. "Latch on to them and find out their secrets. How are they able to show these houses and convert them to sales? Is it the way they look or the words they say? Perhaps they've built up their network through good old-fashioned conversations and genuine friendships? What do you think?"

Allie Swanson raised her hand. She had one year under her belt as an agent with a pitiful closing percentage. Jamal felt like she could use a mentor, but the team would rather drop dead than take on the burden. "What about the properties that they sell? And their leads? Does that have anything to do with it?"

"Of course, dummy," Renee said under her breath. Chauncey snickered.

"That has something to do with it," Ashraf said. "But not all the time. Take the house that Jamal is selling. His top three competitors have attempted to move it and all of them failed. Why?"

"Because the place is cursed," Renee said. Ashraf and a few others laughed. Renee, Tim, and Chauncey didn't.

"I don't know about that," he said, "but you are all competent, successful real estate agents, so what's the mystery? What is it about this property that turns people off from buying it? Jamal, do you have an answer?"

"No, I don't," Jamal said. "The place is clean, aside from all the junk you guys left in the basement. Thanks for that." Tim and Renee smirked. Chauncey pretended not to hear. "And there are upgrades to the appliances, the floors, and the windows. I can't see a reason why it won't sell in a week or two," he said.

"See? A week or two is all it will take for him to move it. Jamal believes he will sell it, and sometimes Allie, that's all it takes. A person must have strong faith, then they can do their best to fight whatever stands in their way and win. Without the proper way of thinking, you will defeat yourself. And," Ashraf said, "you will be stuck in a mediocre office the size of a closet near the bathroom."

After the meeting, Jamal sat down in his office. Beyond the

window, a sea of women marching into the banquet hall caught his eye. His reception had been held there. He and Qaylah kept theirs quaint since her family didn't attend. It ate him up, seeing her suffer like that. He took solace in her finding kindness in his parents.

Jamal scanned the crowd. It didn't look like a wedding. His eyes darted from one person to the next, searching for clues, landing on an unusually dark-skinned woman in bright red clothing. A loose, lacy veil draped her head, obscuring her eyes, but something about her suggested she could see him through the glass. A chill ran up his spine.

She spread her hands out in front of herself like she held a ball. The other women turned and faced the window, mimicking her pose. Hairs on Jamal's neck prickled. The woman in red twisted her hands in a quick, jerking motion. The other women did the same.

"What the hell?"

Two knocks on the door stole his attention. "Busy?" Saalih Ashraf peeked his head inside the office.

"No, Saalih, come in, please." Jamal glanced out the window again. The women filed into the banquet hall like nothing had happened. He didn't see the woman wearing red. He shrugged it off and rose from his chair as if he were greeting a foreign dignitary.

Jamal figured Saalih was in his late forties or early fifties, but he didn't feel comfortable asking. Ashraf didn't carry himself like an old man, but Jamal showed him deference as he would for an older uncle. When he sat down, Jamal placed a cup of tea in front of him. Jamal didn't like chai, but he kept it brewing in case the boss stopped by. He was a salesman after all; the little things made all the difference. "Is something wrong, Saalih?"

"Nothing big," Ashraf said, playing with the zipper on his jacket. "How are things? Is everybody treating you well?"

"Yeah, same as always," Jamal said. Why wouldn't they?"

"No reason. Hannah told me you hurt your hand," his boss said, nodding towards the double-bandaged digit on Jamal's hand. "She said it looked bad."

"It's fine. I cut it on a piece of pottery. I assume one of those clowns tossed it into the mailbox. It fell, and I picked it up from the broken side by mistake."

"Okay. If it gets worse, go to a doctor."

"I will," Jamal said, raising an eyebrow. He couldn't believe that Saalih came just to check on his finger.

"I spoke with a couple of people in the office, Jamal. They had some concerns about you praying in the boardroom."

"They did?"

"Yup."

Jamal narrowed his eyes. What did that snob Renee and her punk companion, Chauncey, have to say about his praying? "I made sure the boardroom was empty before I started," Jamal said. "And I wasn't loud about it either."

"I know you wouldn't cause a disturbance in the office, Jamal. I just want everyone to feel comfortable around us. Sometimes when we do something that seems harmless, even when we try our best, it can be off-putting to those who don't understand our lifestyle."

"I usually pray in my office, but I didn't want to miss the meeting." His boss peered across the desk. Even sitting, his six-foot-five frame made Jamal squirm. "If you think it's best, I'll be more discreet."

"I'm glad to know that you're a team player, Jamal. I've arranged for you to pray with the brothers at the law firm a few doors down, from now on, okay? It's better that we pray together if we can't make it to the masjid, right?"

"That's true, it's better," Jamal agreed. Saalih sounded a lot like Qaylah. He hated nagging.

"Oh, and one other thing. I know you mean well, but someone mentioned your outfits."

"My outfits?"

"Yes. Your outfit, while it is professional and you wear clean and stylish clothing, it doesn't fit in with the local norms. Do you know what I mean?"

Jamal blinked and looked across his desk in disbelief. "You have a problem with my thobe? I always dress them up with blazers and dress pants and I wear nice shoes." Saalih sighed. Jamal kicked himself. He wanted this man's respect, not to sound whiny.

"I agree, Jamal. America should be used to us by now, especially you. You're a young, successful, Black American man who happens to be Muslim. But they aren't ready. Please dress like where you live. This isn't Saudi. Loosen up."

"I like to dress modestly," Jamal said.

"And you will be. Wear a button-down shirt occasionally or throw on some jeans with a nice kurta. It's a looser, Pakistani style." Ashraf looked through the glass walls behind him. "It doesn't scream jihad. Do you know what I mean? Your beard is enough to make some people nervous. Let's not give them reasons to single you out from the pack, okay?"

"You want me to pray somewhere else? Stop wearing my thobe and throw on jeans once in a while?"

Ashraf rose to his feet and headed for the door. "I knew you'd understand, Jamal. Keep this up and Chauncey is going to get nervous about his number one slot. See you later." Jamal sat back in his chair. He looked out the window once again, dumbfounded by the barrage of advice from his boss.

"With all-due respect, Saalih, I don't think so." Jamal

turned his attention back to the pile of contracts on his desk. He was going to get that office and he would do it his way.

A tap at the window caught his attention. Beyond the glass, he saw the woman in red across the banquet hall parking lot. She stared at him through her veil. His finger hurt.

CHAPTER THREE

"As Salaamu Alaikum, I'm home." Jamal tossed his keys into the dish on the entryway table in the foyer and removed his shoes at the door.

"Jamal, Jamal, Wa Alaikum As Salaam." Katie came bounding down the stairs, red, curly hair bouncing from her shoulders.

"There's my sweet girl. Come here, Jellybean." Jamal swept her up in his arms, hugging her and the tattered brown teddy bear, Mister Sniffles, which she refused to clean or replace.

"Salaam, babe, how was your day?" Jamal watched as Qaylah walked in with an exaggerated waddle that wouldn't be real for at least another four months and smiled. He made a mental note to cut her some slack from his teasing; the morning sickness and fatigue were genuine.

"My day was fine," he said, peppering her cheeks and lips with kisses. "What about you two? Did the world treat you with kindness?"

"Yes," Katie said, pulling her bear from between them. "I made a bunch of art out of popsicle sticks and we had cotton candy at school," she said. "But then I fell down at the playground and got a scratch on my elbow, see?" She held up her arm and showed him a tiny bandage with jump roping dinosaurs.

"Oh, I hope you feel better soon," Jamal said, kissing near the bandage. "I got hurt today too," he said, showing them the bandage on his finger.

"Yucky," Katie said, scrunching her face.

"Babe, it's bleeding through the bandage," Qaylah said.

"No, it stopped," he said, wiggling it. He turned over his hand and saw blood oozing out of the bottom of the bandage. "That's strange. It stopped bleeding hours ago," he said.

"Maybe you reopened the cut. Let's go to the kitchen and get it cleaned up," Qaylah put his shoes in the closet and headed for the kitchen.

"Down you go, Jellybean," Jamal said, putting Katie on the floor. He followed Qaylah and joined her at the sink, where she stood with a small kit of bandages and antiseptic.

"We should wash it first, Jamal. Just to clean it up, then we can see what the problem is."

"Yes, Ma'am." He took off the bandage and tossed it into the garbage can. "I guess I opened it up again. It doesn't hurt like it did earlier, and the cut doesn't look large enough for it to keep bleeding."

"You're right," she said, turning on the tap. "Hold it under the water and wash off the excess." He did as she ordered and washed the cut. "Do you think it needs medical attention? It seems like the more you wash it, the more it bleeds."

"No, I'm okay. I think it just needs a little of that germ spray and maybe some ointment to prevent scarring before you bandage it."

"Alright. Monitor it and go to the doctor if it gets worse."

"Thanks, Qaylah," he said, kissing her on the head. "You're a good caregiver."

After they finished, Qaylah served a filling dinner at the

table. Jamal settled in, giving Katie his full attention until bedtime.

"Dinner was excellent, babe. You're getting good at cooking," he said, cuddling with Qaylah on the sofa.

Her head popped up from the crook of his arm, and she gave him a bemused look. "What's that supposed to mean? I've always been able to cook."

"Yeah, but I can tell you put a little soul into those collard greens," he said, smiling. "You got that from my mama."

"Wrong, Jamal Jackson. I got that recipe from Grandma Jean," she said.

"Grandma Jean, huh? She could throw down like that?"

"Yes, she could. Grandma Jean was from the backwoods of Tennessee, and she used to cook the biggest Sunday dinners you could imagine," she said. "And what does a boy from Rhode Island know about collard greens, anyway?"

He flashed a grin at Qaylah. "You've got a point. This Rhode Island boy knows nothing about collard greens or sweet potato pie or pumpkin. Hell, I can't even tell the difference between those two."

"Exactly, so be quiet and let Grandma Jean's family recipes work their magic on you."

"I'll eat Grandma Jean's cooking, but it's Mama Qaylah's magic that's working on me," he said, leaning in for a kiss.

"Now, you're talking."

THE NEXT MORNING, Jamal slipped out of bed and into the shower before work. He had a full day ahead of him, getting the house up to his standards before showing it. The usual team would shampoo the carpets and deliver a few select pieces of furniture throughout the day. The lock on the crawl space needed opening for the air conditioning repair-man, too.

"Good morning, babe. I hope you have time for breakfast," Qaylah said, shoveling scrambled eggs and hash browns onto a plate when he came downstairs.

"Good morning to you too," he said, kissing her cheek. "I do, but I have to hurry. Morning, Jellybean." Katie sat in her chair scooping rainbow-colored cereal into her and Mister Snif-fle's mouths.

"Jamal, who were you talking to last night?" Katie asked.

"You need to pick Katie up from daycare this evening," Qaylah said.

"How come?" Jamal asked. Katie needed to be picked up by five o'clock, and he didn't know if the preparations for the house staging would be completed by then. She'd have to ask his mother instead.

"I told you, I have a prenatal visit with Dr. Simon at four. I won't make it to the daycare by then."

"Qaylah, you know I have to get this house ready. I'm under a lot of pressure to get it sold. I'm trying to make some decent money so that we can get a dream house of our own," he said, biting into his eggs.

"Who were you talking to, Jamal? Mister Sniffles said that he could hear you talking to someone in the kitchen when we went to the bathroom."

"I wasn't in the kitchen last night, Jellybean. Qaylah, what did you put in these eggs?" Jamal asked, spitting them out on the plate.

She furrowed her brow. "Nothing, just salt and pepper with a little garlic powder. Why did you spit it into the plate, babe? That's gross."

"Sorry. I guess they're bad." He got up and scraped the food into the garbage can.

"You were talking about getting a bigger office when you sell the house and how you were going to beat Chauncey's ass."

"Katherine Denise Cavanaugh, what did you say?" Qaylah turned off the stove and marched to the tap. "Get over here, right now." She opened a kitchen drawer and got out a box of soap, then pulled the bar from its packaging and held it in her hand.

Katie's chin dropped to her chest, and she stuck out her lips.

"I'm waiting, Katie. Get over here. Now."

Katie slid down from her chair and approached her mother.

"Open your mouth."

"Qaylah," Jamal began, but didn't finish.

"No, Jamal. She cannot talk like that. Open up." The girl did as she was told, and Qaylah stuck the bar into her mouth.

Jamal winced as he caught Katie's reflection in the toaster, her tiny mouth stretched to its capacity with a white bar of soap hanging more out than in it. "That's enough, Qaylah."

"I'll tell you when she's had enough." Katie gagged and pushed the bar out of her mouth. "Katie, hold on to the soap. Hold it. Put it back in your mouth!" The little girl's face streamed tears as she put the soap back into her mouth.

"That's enough!" Jamal slammed his hand on the table, having forgotten about his cut finger. "Shit," he said, shaking the pain from his hand. Qaylah shot him an incredulous look. He realized his mistake and shook his head. Shit again.

"Forget it, Katie. Go to the bathroom to wash out your mouth," Qaylah said, not breaking the icy stare she gave Jamal. Katie climbed up her step stool and spat the bar into the sink, retching on a mouthful of spit and suds then jumped down and ran to the upstairs bathroom, coughing and sputtering the whole way.

"You were in the kitchen swearing last night," Qaylah said.

"No, I was not in the kitchen. I slept next to you last night and never got out of bed."

"You must have gotten out of bed at some point, Jamal. I know who Chauncey is. What's this talk about kicking his behind?"

"I don't know, Qaylah. I don't recall getting out of bed last night. I don't even remember praying at Fajr time this morning."

"You didn't. I tried waking you, but you didn't get out of bed until an hour ago, after the sun was shining. You missed it."

"Then how could I have been in the kitchen talking about Chauncey? The only reason you know about him is because you met him at the company picnic. Katie didn't come to the picnic."

Qaylah put a hand on her slender hip. Her face tensed, looking tired and wooden. "Maybe you missed Fajr because you were up all night gossiping on the phone or something. Either way, it's obvious you're the one with the potty mouth, Jamal."

"Maybe she remembers hearing swear words from her dad," Jamal said. The mention of Qaylah's ex caused her to wince.

"Don't blame Brian for your inappropriate behavior. Besides, Katie doesn't know him that well. We agreed you wouldn't use that kind of language around Katie because I don't want her using it. I'd appreciate it if you'd stick to your word." She buried her face in her hands.

Taken aback, Jamal crossed the kitchen and pulled her close. "I'm sorry, baby. I didn't think about how it would make you feel. Don't cry, Qaylah, I'm not like him," he said, holding her close. "I'm not like him at all. I love you and I'm crazy about Katie, too. You're both going to live your best lives with me." He smoothed down the stray blonde hairs on her head and kissed the top of it. He listened to her sniffle as she leaned into him.

"Alright," she said, wiping her eyes. "I forgive you."

"I have to go," he said. "I'm gonna fix up this cute little house and make us some nursery money. Then you can arrange it any way you like." He kissed her on the lips, then grabbed his phone and keys off the counter. "As Salaamu Alaikum. Tell Jellybean I'll see her this evening."

"Wa Alaikum As Salaam," she replied, following him to the door. "Jamal?"

"Yes?" He tied his shoes, then stood to his full height.

"I hope you kick his butt," she said, smiling.

"That's my girl." With Qaylah's blessing, he headed out the door to kick Chauncey's ass. No matter how she watered it down, that's what she had meant.

CHAPTER FOUR

"WHAT THE FUCK?" Jamal drove his Escalade into the driveway on Spiegel Road. If this was someone's idea of a prank, he didn't find it amusing. There were sick people in the world, and then there were people who did inexplicable shit like this.

Birds blanketed every inch of the front lawn. All black. All dead. Crows. Smeared blood coated the wooden porch and front door, along with strange black symbols.

Jamal took out his phone and called the police station, then his boss.

"Who would do something like that?" Ashraf asked. "It sounds like something my mother told me from back home. A curse or black magic."

"I don't know what it is, but the police are sending someone to investigate. I need to contact the insurance company, but I can't do that until I fill out a police report. I'll also need landscaping to come by as well as a painter. I can't believe this."

"Do what you've got to do," Ashraf said. "Be quick about it; we don't want to turn away any potential buyers."

Jamal sat in his car and made phone calls to several contractors, hoping he'd get someone asap. He confirmed the time with the insurance agent, and a squad car pulled behind him while he was on the phone. A tall white officer with jet black hair walked up and tapped his window.

"Good morning," the cop said. "I'm Officer Jack Parker. Are you the one who called the station?"

"Yep. That was me. I don't know if I'd call it a good morning, but I hope it's going well for you," Jamal said.

"This is your place? What the hell happened?" Officer Parker surveyed the mess on the grass and gritted his teeth.

"No, I'm the real estate agent from Ashraf Realty," he said, pointing to the sign. "I haven't been inside the property yet, or off the sidewalk for that matter. Can you check it out and make sure it's safe to enter the house?"

"What time did you arrive?" The cop said, looking over Jamal's credentials.

"About ten minutes ago. I was about to clean up inside but found this disgusting mess waiting for me. I've never seen anything like it."

"Can you think of anyone who would do something like this? Someone trying to sabotage you?"

"Nobody comes to mind," Jamal said, pushing his list of office rivals out of his head. They wouldn't stoop this low, would they?

The cop shrugged. "It just strikes me as strange that someone would go to all the trouble to deface the property of an uninhabited house."

"I agree," Jamal said, taking back his identification.

"Sit tight, I'll check out the place. Do you have a key?"

"Yeah, let me get it for you," he said, fishing the key out of his pocket. "It's this one right here. The other ones are for the back door, and the crawl space has a padlock on it."

"Thanks. I'll be back in a few. If you see anything strange, honk your horn."

Jamal watched Officer Parker walk towards the house, inspecting dead crows along the way. He then stepped over the symbols drawn on the porch steps and climbed to the top. Once he unlocked the door, he disappeared inside.

Jamal craned his neck out of the car window but couldn't get a proper view inside the windows. He climbed out and leaned against the side of the vehicle, waiting for a sign of the officer. A clicking noise caught his attention. The small black dog from yesterday trotted down the neighbor's sidewalk, then onto the grass. He didn't waste any time sniffing and licking the bird carcasses.

"Hey, stupid, get away from that. You don't know where it's been. Hey." The dog paid him no attention, choosing to nibble at the birds instead. A sickly crunch sounded as he crushed bird skulls with his jaw.

Jamal stepped away from the Cadillac and checked for the neighbor. The guy was a prick, but that didn't mean he didn't have a right to know what his pet was doing. "I'm gonna go get your owner," Jamal said to the dog. "You better not die while I'm gone." He crossed the yard and knocked on the front door.

"YEAH, WHAT DO YOU WANT, HOMEBOY?" The guy stood at the door in a white t-shirt and boxers, the kind with the peephole at the front. Jamal turned away before his eyes caught something he regretted.

"Somebody trashed the yard next door with dead birds. Your dog is trying to eat them," Jamal said.

"What? Who did it?" The man said, stepping onto his porch. Jamal stepped back, waving away the stench of cigar smoke and liquor.

"I have no idea. There's a cop checking it out, but your dog is trying to eat the birds. If I were you—"

"You ain't me, are you, boy?" The man got into Jamal's personal space. "If you think you can come over here and sell houses in my neighborhood to one of your kind, you're mistaken. I won't stand for any more degenerates living here."

Jamal eyed the man. "Where did that come from? I walked over here to warn you about your mutt, and you want to play redneck now? Forget this. I hope he chokes." He scrambled down the porch stairs with the man hot on his heels. Jamal quickened his pace, not interested in the man's next play.

"You'd like that, wouldn't you, Muzzie? If my innocent little pooch got hurt from something that you probably had a hand in, that would turn you on, wouldn't it?"

"Get lost, you old geezer. I don't have time for this." Jamal crossed back into the yard, avoiding dead crows, and got into his vehicle. The man grabbed Jamal's door and wedged his body in the way. "Get the fuck out of here, you crazy sonofabitch."

"Get out of my neighborhood." The man grabbed at Jamal's arm and found himself flat on the pavement.

"Knock it off, Tobias." Jamal and the neighbor paused as Officer Parker closed the front door and stepped down from the porch. "Leave the man alone, Tobias. He's selling houses, not drugs."

"He let Buck eat those damned things on the lawn," Tobias said.

"Come on, Tobias, take your dog and go on home. Mister Jackson was trying to do you a favor."

"I don't need favors from his kind, and how do you know he didn't kill those birds himself? He was sore at Buck yesterday after he whizzed on his tires. You don't know what he's capable of doing."

"I doubt he'd do something that drastic to get at your dog. The little bastard deserves a kick in the ass, but he doesn't deserve all this. Now, move along." Officer Parker looped his fingers in the belt around his hips and waited. The older man picked himself up, scooped up his dog, and stomped across the yard with it tucked under his arm like a football.

"Is there damage inside the house?" Jamal asked. The thought of extensive damage to the interior made him feel queasy. The situation was out of the ordinary as it was. He didn't need more drama. This was supposed to be an easy sell.

"Nope. The house is pristine on the inside, and the back-yard is clear, too. How'd you hurt your hand?" Officer Parker asked.

"This? I cut it yesterday on a piece of pottery."

"Is that right? It looks nasty. You might wanna visit a doctor. Did you see anything suspicious while I was inside?"

"Like what?" Jamal asked.

"I don't know. Cars driving by or someone taking a slow walk down the street? People who do twisted stuff like to admire their work. Or at the very least, they like to check out the victim's reaction."

Jamal shook his head. "I didn't notice anybody. I saw the dog nosing around in the mess and went straight next door."

"If you can think of anything else or you need me, call the number on my card or dial nine-one-one if it's an emergency."

"Am I free to get this place cleaned up?"

"We'll get someone from animal control to round up the birds, but I don't see why you can't take care of the rest. The sooner, the better. It's gonna be quite a job, by the looks of it."

Jamal sighed. "I think you're right. Should I be worried about the neighbor—Tobias?"

"Nah. He likes to get a rise out of people, but he's harmless."

"Yeah, and he's a bigot."

"Let it go, Mister Jackson. He hates every living soul, except that damn mutt of his. Ignore him and don't engage. Even if you think you're helping him, he'll turn it around and make you regret it. Anyway, I've got to head out, and it looks like you've called the cavalry to help you fix this mess, so take this report for the insurance company and have yourself a nice day."

"Thanks." Jamal took the yellow slip of paper and tucked it into a manilla folder inside his bag. When the officer drove off, the atmosphere shifted. The wind blew and the wings of the crows flapped. Jamal checked up and down the street, searching for the pair of eyes he felt on his back. There was no one around but him and the swaying willow trees. He thought he heard the creak of a rope.

TWO HOURS LATER, Jamal sat inside the house massaging his temples, ignoring the grumbling complaints of his empty stomach. Ashraf's insurance company took extensive photographs of the property and cut him a check for the damages.

The contractor had come and assessed the defiled exterior of the porch and walls, then decided on a color for the exterior paint. The entire porch would have to be redone, and the walkway needed a good power washing to rid the surface of bird blood. The steppingstones needed replacing.

The painter estimated three days for the job, and his landscapers couldn't come until tomorrow, killing his estimated timeline. He couldn't show the house to anyone in this state.

His cellphone inched across the dining table as it rang. He reached out in the nick of time to grab it before he lost it over the edge. "Hello?"

"As Salaamu Alaikum, babe. How're you doing?" Qaylah breathed into the phone with deep, ragged breaths. He could hear traffic noises in the background and crowds of people talking.

"Wa Alaikum As Salaam. It's good to hear your voice right now."

"What's wrong?" She asked.

"Somebody did some gross stuff to the outside of the house, and I had to call in some contractors to clean it up."

"Gross stuff? What'd they do?"

"There are dead birds and blood all over the lawn and on the porch."

"Oh my God, why would someone do that? Did they break in?"

"No, and I'm thankful to Allah for that. There were no signs of tampering inside or in the backyard, but it's throwing me off schedule."

"I'm sorry to hear that."

"Are you outside? I thought your appointment was later this afternoon?"

"It was. The doctor's office called and bumped up my schedule, so I called a taxi to pick me up. I can swing by and pick up Katie to give you a little extra time, but you'll need to come and get us so that we can go grocery shopping. Cab rides are too expensive."

"I can do that, InshaAllah. Listen, Qaylah, I have to get going. Someone from the office is on the other line."

Jamal shivered in his seat. The temperature in the house seemed to fall ten degrees in a matter of seconds. He tried reaching the air conditioner repairman three times this morning, but no one had returned his call. Time was of the essence; if the guy didn't want to be paid, Jamal would find someone else who did.

"Okay, honey, don't forget to pick us up."

"I won't. As Salaamu Alaikum," Jamal said, reaching for his jacket.

"Wa Alaikum As Salaam. I love—"

"Hello? Jamal?" Jamal heard the woman's voice on the other end of the phone but could not match it with anyone he knew. The number on the call display was from a line in the office, but she didn't sound like either of the administrative assistants or the front desk receptionist.

"Hi, who's this?"

"It's Allie. Allie Swanson. From work?"

"Allie?" Jamal stifled a groan. "Oh, right, Allie, how are you?"

"I could be better, Jamal."

"What's wrong?" he asked.

"Are you busy right now? Like, can you steal away for lunch?"

"I'm kind of stuck here while I get the house ready for a showing. There was an incident earlier," Jamal said.

"Yeah, I heard about that," Allie said.

"You did? How? It just happened."

"Chauncey and Renee were talking about it in the break room. Everybody knows now. People are placing bets that they did it."

Jamal clenched his jaw. It made perfect sense. Sabotage.

"Are you still there?" Allie asked. "Jamal?"

"I'm here, Allie. What did you need again?"

"I was talking to Mister Ashraf this morning, and he said that if I don't sell a house by the end of the month, he's going to fire me."

Jamal raised an eyebrow and shrugged. He couldn't say that he was surprised. "I'm sorry to hear that, Allie. It's a tough business. Do you have any leads that you can sway? If you have people on the fence, they might come through for you if they like you."

"Can we meet in person for lunch? I need to pick your brain about a few things."

"I don't know, Allie. I've got a lot of things to take care of here at the house."

"Aren't you waiting for the contractors anyway? Come on, Jamal, I'm desperate. It's my treat," she said.

"Allie, I don't know."

"If you don't help me, I'll lose everything. You're the best, Jamal, and there's so much that I can learn from you. I need your help. I'll make it up to you, I promise."

She seemed like a good person. Jamal recalled that his first days in the office were shaky too. His mood shifted. Women in anguish made him uneasy. In the back of his mind, Jamal heard Qaylah telling him to be charitable. *Fine.* Allie needed help. So be it.

"Alright, Allie. Where should we meet?"

"I reserved a spot at Hailey's Bistro at Potomac Mall. I'll meet you there in fifteen minutes."

CHAPTER FIVE

"You know, you could totally be an actor."

"I've never heard that before," I said cracking a smile. The lunch rush at Hailey's Bistro was insane. Jamal appreciated Allie for reserving a table. Her infectious smile helped subdue his nerves and ease the tension after his early morning shock.

"I don't know why not. You've got that look. By the way, I was going to come here with or without you," she said, as they sat down at a small booth in the middle of the packed restaurant. "They have the best food in town."

"I haven't been here before," Jamal said, looking at the menu.

"Oh, God. I am sorry, Jamal. I didn't think about you having dietary restrictions. Forgive me for being insensitive," she said, smacking her forehead. "Should we go somewhere else?"

"No, don't worry about it, Allie. They have fish options, so it's all good."

"Are you sure?"

"I'm sure," he said, sipping on a glass of water the waitress set down for him earlier. "It's nice of you to bring it up. Most people don't think about it at all until they're chomping on bacon in front of me," he said, smiling.

"I used to be a vegan, so I know how important it is to make sure you can eat something when you go out with friends. Otherwise, the meal will be a real bummer."

"What made you want to be a vegan? Was it about animal rights, or health?"

"Affordability. I was living on very little at one point in my life," she said, playing with a plastic straw. "I had to account for every dollar and cent. Sometimes it would come down to having enough money to buy food or pay the electric bill."

"I'm sorry to hear that," he said.

A server approached the table with his pad in hand. "Hi, I'm your server, Phil. What can I get for you folks today?" He sat a basket of long, thin breadsticks on the table between them with a small bowl of whipped butter.

"I'll have the steak salad with a baked potato, and an iced tea," Allie said, passing her menu to the server.

"I'll have grilled tuna and mixed vegetables," Jamal said.

"And to drink?"

"Whatever carbonated water you have on hand," he said, giving back the menu.

"Okay, that should take about ten to fifteen minutes. I'll be right back with your drinks." He walked away and Jamal grabbed a breadstick from the basket. He felt ravenous after the strange-tasting eggs that Qaylah had cooked for breakfast.

"Thank you for agreeing to meet with me, Jamal. I'm in over my head, but I want to go out fighting. This may sound dramatic, but if I don't accomplish my goals, I'm leaving town. I couldn't stand the humiliation if I stayed."

Jamal shrugged. "Losing a job is serious, but it's not everything. If you don't sell a house, so what? If real estate isn't the right career, move on to something else. Or think about how you can use your real estate license to do other things."

"Like what?"

"Teach people the legalities of flipping houses. You could hold classes all over the city. Prepare others for the exam. There are lots of options."

"Yeah, but I'm passionate about this. I love handing the keys over to a new homeowner. Houses mean something, Jamal. It's more than just a place to lay your head at night. Home ownership is epic. You can leave a legacy for your children. My daddy said, 'If you don't own a piece of land, you don't own nothing.'"

"You're right," Jamal said, nodding. "What's your plan? How do you plan to sell a house between now and the end of the month?"

She threw her head back against the booth's padded chair. "I don't know. I've held open houses for both properties they assigned me, and people are streaming in all hours of the day to look at them, but no one seems interested. I can't convert them." Jamal watched her freckled throat constrict as she spoke with her head back. He caught himself staring and forced his eyes down to the table.

"You make it sound like a religion," Jamal said, shoving a breadstick into his mouth.

"It's not at all," she laughed. "I'm passionate about it because of how hard things were growing up."

She sat up and looked thoughtful for a moment before she continued. "We weren't poor by any means, but my mom and dad split up and sold the house to a distant family member. Then, that family member did the same thing. My folks said the property was cursed and that nobody was ever going to stay in that house long. I promised myself that when I grew up, I was going to buy it and keep it forever, and nobody was going to rip it out of my hands."

"Did you buy it?" Jamal asked. Phil showed up as Allie was about to answer and sat their drinks on the table.

"No, I live in a house near Calliope Falls River. Buying the house was a childhood fantasy. Everyone who lived there suffered. Maybe I should buy it and raze the damned thing."

Jamal nodded. "I don't know if you're religious, but you could turn that negativity into something positive if you have the house blessed."

"I am, in my own way," Allie said. "I'll think about it if I end up changing my mind."

"It can't hurt. My wife had our house blessed. She said she prayed that any evil introduced to the house would destroy itself."

"Here you go, folks. Steak salad and grilled tuna," Phil said, placing their respective dishes on the table a few moments later. "If you need anything, let me know. Enjoy your meal." He scurried away and the two of them dug into their lunches.

"So, tell me," Allie said, swallowing a bite of her salad, "what do you think my course of action should be to get one of these houses sold?"

"Well, where are the properties?" Jamal asked.

"Ashbury," Allie said.

Jamal stopped cutting his tuna. "Ashbury Heights? You can't move properties in Ashbury? Allie, people have gotten into fistfights just to view houses in that neighborhood. What's up?"

Her eyes welled up with tears. "I know that I'm the problem, Jamal. You're nicer than everybody gives you credit for, not like Chauncey and Tim. I asked them for help, but Tim brushed me off in front of everyone, and Chauncey said that I should go stand in the welfare line."

Jamal's face darkened. "You asked Tim and Chauncey before me? What about Renee? Or Hannah? She's a receptionist, but she might know something about houses. After all, she lives in one." He knew that he sounded salty, but he felt like an idiot. She'd asked him third, after being rejected and humiliated by Chauncey and Tim. Tim, who tied for third place in office sales with Renee.

Allie's hands covered her eyes. "That sounded horrible, didn't it, Jamal? I'm sorry. I wanted to ask you for help first, but I didn't want to take up your personal time. You are a newlywed, right?"

"Yes, I am. I would have helped you, Allie. All you had to do was ask. In fact, that's what you need to do as a realtor for every house you sell when you can't move it. Ask your network for help," Jamal said.

"I'm new; I don't really have a network. Or work friends."

"Do you think I got where I am by having work friends? A network is more than that. You carry your business cards around for a reason. You want to make an impression on people and leave them with something tangible. When you strike up a conversation with someone at the supermarket, tell them what you do and tell them you can help them find what they're looking for. Use what you know to your advantage, Allie." He watched her pull out her phone and open the notes app.

"I know real estate laws and how to read from scripts," she said.

"That's no good. Tear up your scripts and use what's in your heart. Tell people the story about the little girl Allie who lost her house and wants to get it back for her family. Move people. It may not work with everyone, but someone out there will remember Allie Swanson, the real estate agent."

"You make it sound like I'm curing cancer," she said.

"You're not doing all that. But you said it yourself. You're setting up a legacy for somebody's family."

"Okay. I have to approach as many people as I can and

strike up a conversation. Won't that seem a little creepy? 'Hi, I'm Allie, the realtor. I want to sell you a house.'"

"That's kind of obnoxious, but not creepy. You want to build rapport with people. Talk to them like they mean something and genuinely listen to what they have to say. And please, check any shyness you have at the door. If you sound like you know what you're talking about, they'll believe you."

They ate the rest of the meal in a comfortable mix of silence and small talk. He learned that she was the youngest child of six and that her father was a retired coal miner. Her mother died soon after the divorce, and she grew up with a stepmother who brought three children into the mix.

"We were a regular Brady Bunch," Allie said as Phil cleared the table.

"Would you like two separate checks?" He asked, balancing their plates.

"No," Jamal said, taking out his wallet. "I've got this one."

"You don't have to do that, Jamal. It was my idea. I should pay."

"Relax, Allie. I enjoyed the distraction. Let me treat. I'll add it to my taxes as a business meeting," he said, winking. Phil brought the credit card machine. Jamal eyed Phil's wrist. A smudge of makeup revealed a black tattoo barely visible against his dark skin. It looked eerily similar to the statue he'd found in the mailbox at Spiegel Road.

"Is something wrong, Sir?" Phil drew his sleeve over his wrist.

"No," Jamal said, adding the tip before he tapped his card on the display. "Your tattoo. What is it?"

"My grandmother was in a religious order back in the day. When she passed away, I got inked in her honor."

"It looks familiar. What's the name of the religious group?"

"I can't remember. I used to hang at my grandmother's

house sometimes, so she and I were kind of cool, you know? My sisters were really into it, but I was just there to play with my cousins. My mom doesn't talk about it," Phil shrugged.

"Sorry, man. I wasn't trying to bring up bad memories."

"It's all good. You two enjoy the rest of your day." He gave Jamal the receipt and disappeared into the sea of bustling servers. The pit of Jamal's stomach lurched. The call to prayer sounded on his phone, and he turned it off before it called too much attention to their table.

"What's that?" Allie said.

"It's the prayer alert app on my phone. It's telling me that the afternoon prayer has started."

"Do you need to leave?" She asked, rising from the table.

"I have plenty of time," he said, following her out of the restaurant and into the mall.

"Good. Do you think you can help me out a little? Maybe give me some pointers on a few outfits for work?"

"Me? Wouldn't you rather get that kind of information from another woman?"

"Well, you and I are in the same profession, so I don't see how a random woman in a store has a better opinion than my coworker. Please, Jamal? I'm begging you."

She did a lot of that. Jamal was starting to think she had a flair for exaggeration. "I need to get back to the property, Allie."

"This is my last chance to make a good impression on these buyers. I'm giving it all I've got."

"I don't know how I feel about shopping with you, Allie. It seems a little intimate." He thought about what Qaylah would say if she knew he was helping another woman pick out clothing. Somehow, he didn't think she'd let it slide because it was work clothing. His wife wasn't a jealous woman, but she did have an unspoken expectation for respect.

"Jamal, relax. I'll just try them on in the changing room and come out to let you see what they look like. All that you have to do is give me a thumbs up or down." She tilted her head in the same way Katie did when she asked him to sneak a cookie. He grinned from the corner of his mouth.

"I'll give you a half an hour to find what you need, then I have to get back to check on the contractors."

"Thanks, Jamal. You're the best."

"Please stop thanking me all the time, Allie..." A gentle swaying object hung from the rafters caught his eye. Feet. Jamal dropped his eyes.

"What's wrong?" Allie turned and looked up. "Do you see something weird?"

I see a dead woman hanging from the ceiling. She'd think he was crazy if he admitted it. Maybe the money from his next sale should go towards a well-deserved vacation instead of the nursery. "Nah, I thought there was something, but I was mistaken. I'm all yours, Allie. Lead the way."

CHAPTER SIX

"WHAT DO you think of this one?" Allie twirled in a navy pencil skirt and a light pink blouse. She smoothed the skirt against her butt and checked herself out in the mirror.

Jamal sneaked a look, then glanced around the store. He was nervous about this woman. He didn't have friends of the opposite sex, not even his female cousins. It wasn't something that was tolerated in his community. Although he was here out of the goodness of his heart, he hoped no one that he knew saw him. Especially someone who knew his mama. Standing here with Allie, Jamal couldn't make heads or tails of why it felt wrong. He was having a good time helping a coworker. This was charity.

"It fits you like a glove," he said. His face burned.

"Do you think it looks professional? I mean, I'll be wearing a jacket over the skirt with a dark pair of low heels. It's okay to wear this to the office, right?"

"Sure," he nodded. Qaylah didn't dress like that, and he had no clue if it was appropriate for a non-Muslim woman to show that much leg at work or not. This was a bad idea.

"The reason that I'm asking is that I'm single, and don't want to have one set of clothing for work and another for cocktail hour. Know what I mean?"

"Sure," he said again.

Allie laughed. "You don't know what I mean, do you? You probably don't do bars after work, right?"

"No, I don't. I go home to my family after work. I spend so much time away from them, it doesn't seem fair to stay away any longer than I already do."

"That's admirable," she said. "I wish every man was like that. Go to work, come home, and spend time with his family. It may have saved my parents' relationship had he spent time with my mom. Listen to me, being so dreary," she said. "Let me move on to the next one. Oh, wow, look at this." she said, grabbing a shirt off a rack in the men's section. "Jamal, will you please try this on? The blue compliments your brown complexion so well."

"Whoa," he said, holding up his hands. "We didn't come here for me. This is about you."

"I know, but this shirt is perfect for you. Look in the mirror." She held it up under his chin and turned him around. He felt heat rising where she touched his arms. "See? It looks great."

Jamal started to protest but changed his mind. It looked good, and it was his favorite shade of blue.

"You like it, don't you?"

"Yes, I like it. It's a nice shirt," he said, taking it back to the rack.

"What are you doing? Don't put it back." Allie took the shirt from his hand and raced down the aisle. "We need the perfect pair of jeans to balance the look. What size do you need, thirty-two?"

"Thirty-four," he said. "But I'm not here to buy anything, Allie. I came for you."

"And now I'm returning the favor. I want you to take this and try it on while I switch outfits. You said it yourself, Jamal;

you go to work, and you come home. When do you do something for yourself?" She picked out a pair of dark jeans and handed them to him. "The men's fitting room is over there. I'll meet you by the mirrors in five minutes."

~

JAMAL LOOKED at himself in the full-length mirror. He looked good. The jeans fit his long legs without hugging. They felt good; he hadn't worn a pair since he was a child. He leaned towards a preppy style and didn't think jeans fit the aesthetic, but Allie was right. He worked hard to provide for his family. Treating himself to something nice didn't interfere with that.

Jamal drew back the curtains and stepped out from the dressing room. Allie was waiting on the showroom floor in a snug-fitting black dress, but she hadn't noticed him approaching. He watched her ginger curls cascade onto her shoulders as she took down her messy bun and rearranged it. His breath caught in his throat for a moment. She could catch a man off guard if she put forth a little effort. "Hey," he said, clearing his throat.

Her face lit up. "Hey, yourself. You look so good."

"Thanks," he said, beaming. "I don't normally wear jeans, but I like them."

"Good for you. Are you going to buy them?"

"I'm on the fence. Saalih says I should loosen up with my wardrobe choices, so maybe I should. On the other hand—"

"On the other hand, nothing," she said. "You should get the outfit, Jamal, and a few others to go along with it. Changing your look can be freeing."

She winked at him in the mirror. Behind her reflection in the corner of the glass, he thought he saw a woman pass by in a red veil. He looked behind him, but no one was there. Jamal relaxed his shoulders and felt the tension leave his body. If he had time tomorrow, he was going to research vacation spots.

"You know what? You're right."

"I speak from experience," she said. "Tell me. What do you think of this dress?"

"You look sexy in that. I-I mean, is it appropriate for work?" He cleared his throat and tugged at the collar of his shirt. He felt stupid and awkward, like he had in high school when girls asked him out. No one believed that he had remained a virgin until he got married. "I'm sorry. I shouldn't have said that to you. It was out of line."

"No, it wasn't. It made my day. To be honest, it made my week. I just turned thirty on Monday."

"Really? You look way younger than thirty," Jamal said.

"Thank you. I'm guessing you're about twenty-five?"

"Thirty-one almost," he said. "But I've looked the same for a long time. I have to give my parents credit for their good genes," he said, flashing her a smile with his perfect white teeth. As good as his genes were, those miracles had come from a good dentist.

"Ageless and attractive? Some people have all the luck."

As superficial as it was, the compliment made him feel good. Her validation made him certain that Ashraf would approve. With her help, he was going to score another win in the boss's eyes. "Do you need to pray soon?" she asked, checking her watch.

"Don't worry about it," he said. "I can make it up later." He muttered a half-hearted prayer of forgiveness under his breath. Sometimes it was hard to break the momentum. "Let's go find some more clothes."

~

"Oh, my God, were we really in the mall for four hours?" Jamal asked, checking the time on his phone. He stared at the multiple shopping bags in his hands and wondered how much hassle it would be returning all the stuff he bought.

"I couldn't believe it when you wanted to shop all the way to the other side. I haven't done that since I passed my real estate exam." Allie pushed her hair out of her face and smiled at him in wide-eyed wonder. "I think you needed some retail therapy as much as I did."

"I kind of feel like throwing up," he said.

She laughed, showing all of her teeth. "Nope, Jamal, look at me. We shouldn't feel guilty for pampering ourselves. We're both under tremendous pressure right now, and this was our one chance to let loose."

Allie placed a firm hand on his forearm and gave it a shake. Her hand felt warm and comforting against his skin. "Don't beat yourself up for letting off steam."

"Maybe you're right," he said, relaxing a little. He had a feeling Qaylah wouldn't see it that way, but he was a grown man and didn't have to answer to her.

"I'd better get going, I've got a meeting," she said, releasing her grip from his arm.

"Me too," Jamal said. "I've got to pick up my wife and step-daughter. Looks like I might be a little late."

"May the wind carry you to your destination with speed," Allie said. "Bye for now." She wiggled her fingers in a delicate wave and tossed him an intense look.

"Bye." Jamal didn't know how to read her expression, but he'd think it over later. "Allie?"

"Yes?"

"I can help you close the properties." He didn't know why he offered, but it was too late to rescind it.

"You would do that for me?"

"Sure. You'd get full credit, of course."

"Jamal, you have made my day," she said, smiling. She rushed over and grabbed his bicep and gave it a squeeze. He flexed, hoping she didn't notice. "Thank you for being such a sweetheart," she said. "We're gonna do great things together, wait and see. I'll be watching your every move."

"You're welcome, Allie. It's like Saalih said. You need to shadow the right person to get what you want. I'm your man."

CHAPTER SEVEN

TWENTY MINUTES LATER, Jamal broke free of the clogged interstate traffic, and turned into the parking lot of the Tri-Cities Preschool. The lot was empty except for one car. He pulled up beside it and noticed Qaylah's tight face. She opened the door and climbed out of the passenger seat, with Katie sleeping in her arms.

"Thanks, Samantha, I'll see you tomorrow," she said to the woman inside. She walked towards the car and Jamal lowered his window.

"As Salaamu Alaikum, Qaylah. I'm sorry, sweetheart, I got delayed," Jamal said through the window. He climbed out of the car and tried taking Katie from her arms, but Qaylah side-stepped him. He rushed ahead of her and opened the door. His wife put the sleeping girl into the booster chair in the back seat and buckled the harness.

"Qaylah." Jamal said, closing Katie's door. Qaylah climbed into the passenger seat and slammed the door. He checked the back seat. Katie slept on. They traveled in silence, five minutes from the house when he remembered that she wanted to go to the grocery store. She sighed and he turned around without further prompting.

"Which store do you want to go to? Selenium is your

favorite, right?" She didn't answer. "Fine, we'll go to Selenium."

Jamal shifted in his seat, glancing at her from the corner of his eye. He hated being ignored. The silent treatment made him feel invisible. Small. She was ruining the high that he'd had hanging out with Allie.

"There was an incident at the house today. I had to call in some contractors to take care of the mess. I think it's going to delay the sale of the house by at least another few days."

"You told me this earlier on the phone, or don't you remember?" Qaylah asked. She spoke with her head turned towards the window.

"That's right, I remember."

"But you don't remember me saying to pick us up on time, Jamal? Did you also forget that I need to pay the preschool extra each time we're late? They charge us a hundred and twenty dollars."

"I'm sorry, babe. I got distracted. But it's okay because you got there on time," he said.

"Who goes shopping in the middle of the day?" she asked, ignoring him.

Jamal looked in the rearview mirror, remembering the pile of shopping bags on the seat next to Katie. He forgot to put them in the trunk. At least she didn't know he was with Allie.

Jamal drove to the front entrance of the grocery store and dropped off Qaylah. He watched her jerk a cart from the carousel and walk stone-faced through the double doors.

"Be like that," Jamal said.

"Who are you talking to, Jamal?" the tiny voice behind him asked.

"Hey, Jellybean, how are you doing, baby girl?"

"I'm good. Where is Mama?"

"She's in the store. Do you want to go inside and ride in the cart?"

"Yes, please. Mama's mad at you for being late."

"Yes, she is. I think she'll need some time to be mad, and then she'll forgive me. What do you think?"

"Yeah, I guess so. She's not as mad at you as she gets when she's talking about my daddy," she said, lifting her arms when he opened the passenger door and unfastened her seatbelt.

"That's a good sign," Jamal said, hoisting her up on his hip. He closed the door behind him and used the key fob to lock the vehicle. For a moment, he wondered when Katie had heard Qaylah get mad at Brian, but he pushed it aside.

They found Qaylah in aisle four, looking at the boxed casserole kits that Jamal hated. Whenever she was upset, she made stuff that barely passed for food. Jamal made a mental note to order out for dinner as much as possible in the coming week.

"Mama, Mama," Katie climbed down from Jamal's hip and raced to the grocery cart.

"Hey, sweetie. Let Jamal lift you up. I don't want to strain too much," Qaylah said.

"You can't even lift her up anymore?" Jamal asked. The question earned him a show of her backside as she spun on her heels and walked down the aisle without the cart. "Come on, Jellybean. Up you go."

For someone with such a delicate condition, Qaylah strutted up and down the rows, tossing objects in the cart like a speed walking powerlifter in an Olympic heat. Katie didn't mind because it gave her a chance to sneak two boxes of nut-free chocolate chip cookies into the cart.

Jamal felt thankful for the short lines as they checked out the groceries. The couple in front of them had a hand basket.

They could get out without Katie growing antsy and go home. His finger had started throbbing again.

"I spy with my little eye, something that is orange," Katie said.

"Forget it Katie, we're not buying cupcakes," Qaylah said.

"It's okay, let her have one," Jamal said.

"She may not have one, Jamal. It may contain peanuts. Have you also forgotten what she said this morning, thanks to you?"

Jamal gritted his teeth. "Qaylah, it was an accident. She didn't mean to say it, and she didn't hear that from me. I was never in the kitchen last night and I, for certain, wasn't talking to anyone last night except you," he said, shoving the groceries down the automatic conveyor belt.

"Yes, you were," Katie said. "You were in the kitchen walking back and forth and you said—"

"Katherine," Qaylah warned, tapping her debit card on the display of the card reader. "Don't."

"Do you want bags?" The cashier asked, amused by Katie. "I see y'all all the time. She is so precious." The cashier reached for the cupcakes and handed them to Katie. "Don't worry, sugarplum, this kind is nut free." She turned to Qaylah. "It's on me, mama. No charge."

"Thank you, Nina," Jamal said before Qaylah could protest. "And yes, to your question, we'd like bags."

"What do you say, honey?" Qaylah asked. Jamal watched her bottle her anger and flatten her lips into a tight, thin line.

"Thank you," Katie said.

Jamal helped the cashier load the groceries into the bags, while Qaylah hurried outside. He noticed how her walk lost its waddle when she was angry. His lips twitched. "Thanks again," he said to the cashier before catching up with his wife.

"We need to go to the masjid," Qaylah said when he finished packing the trunk with the bags.

He sucked in teeth in displeasure before he could stop himself. "What for? Is there a special program happening?"

"No, Jamal. It's time to pray, Maghrib. Did you forget that too?"

"That's enough, Qaylah. I don't need your funky attitude, alright? I get it. You're upset that I was late, and you had to pay. What more do you want from me? I'm sorry. I'll give back your precious money." He clenched his aching finger in his fist and slammed the trunk shut. They rode in silence.

The mosque parking lot overflowed with minivans and taxis, but Jamal was thankful that he arrived late. The rule was, come late, catch the prayer, get out of the parking lot first.

Jamal unlatched his seatbelt and walked around to the passenger side to help Qaylah and Katie out of the vehicle. Qaylah took her daughter by the hand and pulled her along to the women's entrance of the mosque.

He entered the men's side, stumbling through the door. Jamal doubled over and cupped his hands around his knees, forcing air into his lungs. After he recovered from the sudden lack of oxygen in his body, he looked around for the person who pushed him. No one was in the entryway.

"Whatever," he muttered under his breath. People in religious settings could be rude to the point of astonishment. He'd witnessed that when he traveled to Makkah for Umrah during Ramadan. Nothing was sacred anymore.

Jamal hurried across the tiled seal on the masjid floor and entered the musallah, filling in a gap in the back row beside some other men. Everyone settled in, spreading their arms and feet a comfortable distance. And then he felt queasy.

A sudden wave of chills traveled down his shoulders and up his knees towards his midsection. Jamal let out a slow, deliberate breath as the men bent forward, clasping their knees. They came up and he sucked in air. Everyone dropped to their knees, foreheads to the floor. Jamal couldn't follow. He stood locked in place.

Fear gripped him as he failed to lower himself in prostration, symbolizing his obedience to God. The men sat upright, then dove to the carpet once more, synchronized. *I'm stuck.*

Jamal looked around to see who was watching him. No one was, but he felt a presence. Something invisible opened the center of his back and climbed inside of him, zipping him like a woman's dress. *It's in me!*

When the men rose, the congregant standing next to him gave him a slight nudge in the side with his elbow. *Pay attention to your own prayers, buddy.*

Jamal nudged him back, and joined them in ruku, bending and cupping his hands around his kneecaps. The nausea picked up once more, but this time, his knees bent like the others allowing him to bow in submission to his Lord. But he didn't. Jamal's forehead hovered above the carpet. He began panting.

A deep laugh escaped his lips. His brow furrowed. The voice wasn't his. The men sat up once more. This time, Jamal bent down with them, catching his body with the palms of his hands.

He pushed his forehead towards the plush green carpet but couldn't force himself down. Instead, his body went rigid, and he bent backwards in an unnatural pose. Jamal's mouth opened like someone forced their hands inside. A swift pulling motion ejected his lunch all over three men in front of him. Shouts of fury and disbelief escaped the mouths of the praying men, but Jamal didn't care. As he blacked out, he sighed with relief. It was out.

CHAPTER EIGHT

"Maybe you should take a few days off, Jamal. It's obvious that you're sick." Qaylah sat at the dining table when Jamal rushed down the stairs to join the family for breakfast. He had gotten a good night's sleep and wanted to get back to work in haste.

He couldn't wait to see his new wooden sign posted in the front yard, along with the fresh grass blanketing the ground. The day was going to be perfect.

"I'm fine, Qaylah. I felt a little off yesterday, that's all." He reached over to tousle Katie's hair. She pulled away from him and clutched her teddy bear.

"A little off? Jamal, you threw up on people in the masjid and passed out. I'd say that's a little more than off. You look tired, babe."

"Well, I told you those eggs you cooked me were bad," he said.

Qaylah glanced at his legs and drew back. "What is that? Are you wearing jeans, Jamal?"

"Yes. I picked them up yesterday at the mall." He fixed his posture and turned to the back. "They look good on me, don't they? Do you like them, Qaylah?"

She frowned. "Where are your thobe and kufi?"

He turned around. "Upstairs," he said, checking his watch. He didn't have time to get into it with her over what he wore. It was his choice.

"Shouldn't you put them on to cover your awrah? Proper Muslims don't go outside exposing their butt and thighs, but you know that already," she said, carrying her plate to the sink.

... the one who opens himself up to sin becomes vulnerable...

"What's that you're listening to on the computer?" Jamal asked, changing the subject. Qaylah had been listening to religious lectures nonstop for the past few weeks.

How much constant worship did it take to make a person snap? Did she spend her time thinking about anything else? When did she live her life? He'd call his mom when he found the time and ask her to look out for Qaylah.

"It's a lecture on the dangers of jinn possession," Qaylah said. She dug into her bowl of cereal.

Jamal grabbed a bowl for himself, then poured in the milk and ate it standing at the counter. "Why does this sound familiar? Who is the speaker?"

"Ustadh Jones-Ali. He held a lecture last week, but we missed it. You were working late, and I had terrible morning sickness, so I didn't attend. Your mother gave me this recording."

"Reggie Jones-Ali?"

"Uh huh. Do you know him?"

"Yes. We went to RHU together. He majored in accounting. What business does he have, giving Islamic lectures?"

Reggie Jones-Ali, formerly Jones, was a student that Jamal ran into regularly when he attended classes at Rosewood Hollow University. That was before Jamal dropped out and got his real estate license.

Jamal learned early on that Reggie liked the sound of his own voice. Unfortunately, others liked it as well. Jamal thought

Reggie would have gone into entertainment before becoming a speaker on religious tours.

What made him qualified to speak? Reggie was the guy who took extra yoga and reiki classes as filler credits to 'round out his religious consciousness.'

"He's an excellent speaker. I like what he has to say," Qaylah said.

Jamal stopped eating. "Say about what?"

"Many things. He studied under a sheikh in Morocco for the past four years."

"So?"

"He also has a Ph.D. in religious exorcisms."

"Okay. Why are you listening to a recording about exorcisms?"

"Why wouldn't I? It's a part of our faith and since I'm still new to it, I want to learn all that I can about everything."

"It's stupid to waste time on things you don't need to know," Jamal said.

"What's gotten into you, Jamal? You seemed gung-ho about me learning when I converted, but you haven't encouraged me to learn, nor have you taken it upon yourself to teach me."

"Yeah, but Reggie? Seriously? What do you see in him?"

"*See in him*? I'm listening to his lecture. You sound jealous. He's giving valuable information for free from the kindness of his heart. Am I missing something?"

Jamal opened his mouth wide and shoved in the spoon. "Whatever, Qaylah, you do you, I have to go," he said with a mouthful of cereal. He got up from the table and tossed the bowl into the sink.

"As Salaamu Alaikum," Qaylah said.

"Yeah, see you later."

IN THE CAR, Jamal thought about Qaylah's behavior. He didn't like her watching Reggie's lectures. *Listening.* Whatever.

As a Black man, Reggie embarrassed Jamal. His culture seeped through, whereas Jamal blended in. Jamal made sure to practice proper diction and code switched in mixed company. Reggie spoke like he was from the lower-class hoods. In short, he was ghetto. Jamal didn't want anyone associating him with that behavior.

It was true that he hadn't contributed to Qaylah's religious education since she converted. But he didn't need to. What purpose did she have besides serving her husband and children? Certainly not exorcizing the jinn.

People thought Reggie was charismatic and handsome, but what else did he bring to the table? Who did he think he was, calling himself a sheikh? It takes a long time to learn and practice the foundation of the faith—a lifetime could pass without having scratched the surface. Jamal believed the most extraordinary thing about Reggie was that he was a Black man on the Islamic lecture circuit. A novelty.

He turned into the driveway on Spiegel and breathed a sigh of relief. "My boys came through," he said, parking. He cut the engine and hopped out to inspect the work. The sign and the grass looked great.

He glanced at the picture on the sign and frowned. Saalih was right. His image screamed one thing. *Foreigner. I look like an extremist.* Jamal tapped the sign, rocking it back and forth on the hinges.

This look wouldn't do if he were going to be a major player in Saalih's agency. He'd have to take a new headshot and this time, he'd choose a non-Muslim photographer who could make him look more modern and friendly to the public.

Satisfied with the yard, he strolled up the sidewalk, searching for signs of bloody feathers and black paint. The guys in Saalih's crew were solid; they also planted new flowers and hedges that were brighter and fuller, making the curb appeal that much more alluring. The porch smelled of fresh paint, and they updated the mailbox without needing to be told. Today was turning out better than he had hoped.

The phone rang. "Hello?"

"Hey, Jamal, this is Kevin, from Williamson Air Conditioning."

"What's up, man? Did you swing by here yesterday? Something came up and I couldn't be here to let you inside the house," he said, opening the front door.

The interior was bright but a little stuffy from being closed all night. He walked over to the thermostat and turned on the air conditioner. A pleasant breeze hit him in the face, and he relaxed.

"I came by, but there was no need to go inside. The unit was working properly. I can come back in a half hour to check on it if you still have problems, but I don't see any reason to do that."

"I'll tell you what, Kevin, I'm inside the house right now. Everything seems fine today. If I have any more issues, I'll give you a ring, okay?"

"You got it," Kevin said. "Talk to you later, champ."

Jamal hung up and sat his bag on the dining room table. He brought a change of clothes with him in his gym bag so that he wouldn't ruin his new ones. He took them upstairs to the master suite bathroom and began changing. Jamal folded his jeans and slid them onto a silky pink hanger that he borrowed from Qaylah's closet, wrapped his new blue shirt around it, then hung it up.

Jamal jumped backwards, startled by his reflection in the

mirror. The person staring back at him looked ten years older. *What happened to my face?* He opened his gym bag and rifled around inside.

"There you are," he said, pulling out a pair of clippers. He walked into the bathroom and plugged them into the socket next to the sink. "You need a little help," he said to his reflection. "Let me make you look like a winner."

He flipped the switch and hair tumbled down his cheeks and chin into the sink's basin. In a manner of minutes, he had a neat haircut and contour to complement the five o'clock shadow framing his sculpted jaw. "There you are Jamal. I knew you were in there somewhere."

For the rest of the afternoon, everything went by without a hitch. The temperature felt normal again, and he dusted the furniture and arranged a few area rugs to his liking.

The crew returned with the metal junk container and rid the basement of the boxes and trash except for a couple. When they left, he took the broom and mop downstairs to clean the floors and see what was left.

A scratching sound behind a wall diverted his attention. Jamal approached the wall next to the dryer and listened. It was stronger there.

He knelt before the wall and placed his hand against it. His first impression was mice, which weren't impossible, but unlikely since pest control had done an inspection. The scratching sound was too loud to be a mouse. Jamal tapped at it. It tapped back at him.

He put his ear to the wall and listened. The noise stopped. He waited. Hearing nothing, Jamal chalked the whole thing up to his imagination. Leaning on the broom, he waited another minute then continued sweeping.

It took more time than he expected. Jamal swept along the

baseboards and ended up near the awkward corners surrounding the stairs. He stuck the broom into a corner near them and dragged a small object out of the darkness into the light.

"What are you still doing here?" He bent down and picked up the broken clay figurine from the floor. He guessed the cleanup crew had missed it, whatever it was. Curiosity got the best of him. What was it? He tossed it into a small box near the washer. It would have to wait. He was here to sell the house, not research its contents.

The floor tiles shone like new and smelled of fresh pine needles. Everything looked great. He went upstairs to the main floor and lit a few scented candles for the open house. Right after closing a sale, setting up for the showcase was his favorite part.

He puffed the coordinated sofa pillows, styled the coffee table, and dusted bookcases. It was coming together until his bandage stuck to the welcome placard on the main table.

"Damn." He yanked off the bandage and tossed it into the garbage. His finger, swollen and purple, hurt more than he thought it should, but it wasn't bleeding.

He kept going, attaching business cards to a stack of welcome letters, then sat them on gold marbled trays in strategic spots around the house. Jamal was ready to make money. His grandmother said an itchy hand meant that money was coming. He wasn't superstitious like her, but he welcomed it all the same.

Jamal carried his cleaning supplies outside, hurrying down the front steps. When he reached the bottom, he stopped dead in his tracks. "What the fuck are you doing?"

Feces covered the entire front end of his vehicle. The little dog from next door dragged his butt, rubbing shit up and down the windshield. When he finished, the mutt scooted onto the roof of Jamal's white Cadillac, smearing the sunroof from one side to the other.

Stunned, Jamal stared at the dog. It stopped scooting across the hood long enough to stare back. He swore it smiled at him. The dog grew bored of the exchange and broke eye contact. It resumed wiping its ass, heading in the direction of the back window.

"You little sonofabitch, get down from there!" Jamal grabbed the broom and charged the vehicle from the side, careful not to soil himself. "Get down! I'm gonna knock your head off."

The little dog shrank from Jamal, retreating to the far corner of the roof, shaking. Jamal circled the vehicle to get a better angle and swung at the animal, missing by a hair. Buck barked a warning and bared his little teeth. Jamal swatted at him again. "You think you can scare me, mutt? Come over here and try something. I will knock your teeth down your throat."

"Hey, what the hell are you doing to my dog? What's wrong with you chasing a defenseless animal like that? Come on down, Buck." Tobias walked across the grass, his wiry frame draped in a bathrobe and not much else.

The dog tucked his tail between his legs and lowered his head, whimpering and shaking. "Look what you've done," Tobias said. "You scared him, you cocksucker. I should call the cops on you."

"On me? Look what your fucking dog did to my car?" Jamal's body went rigid from head to toe. He restrained himself so he didn't knock the older man's teeth down his throat, too. Adrenaline carried him to the front of the vehicle. "Come around here and look at the shitty hood and the shitty windshield. Look at his fucking shitty feet. He shit all over my car."

"Good. I wish he had gotten the back window too. Come

down, boy, he won't hurt you while I'm here. I'm a registered gun toting American. *Ex-military.*"

The dog whimpered and looked from Jamal to his owner and back again. "He knows better than to mess with me, Buck. Come on, boy." After a long pause, the dog jumped down into Tobias's arms, shit-stained feet, and all. "I mean it, slick. I don't care if my dog shits on your wife's lap. If I see you near Buck again, I won't hesitate to shoot you." Jamal watched the older man carry the dog across the lawn and into his house.

"Motherfucker!" Jamal threw the broom across the yard, hitting his likeness on the sign. The call to prayer sounded on his cellphone. He reached inside and silenced it. Now was not the time for praying. His car needed cleaning. He went back inside, blew out the candles and canceled the open house. Again.

CHAPTER NINE

AFTER HOSING DOWN THE VEHICLE, Jamal ran it through an automatic car wash three times to make sure it was free of dog feces. His anger towards Tobias and his mutt made it hard to focus. When he felt the car couldn't become any cleaner, he drove to the office.

He didn't enjoy spending a lot of time in the office during the day. Nighttime was for contracts and cold calling. The day was for showing houses. The exception was when he made cold calls to the immediate and surrounding neighborhood about an open house, though he could do that from the house on Spiegel or his own home too.

Saalih's car was in the parking lot. He worked seven days a week, except for the two Eid holidays and two weeks for vacation. Jamal wondered when he spent time with his family.

On his way to his office, Jamal spied an older agent, Courtney, gossiping with Renee and Tim in the break room. They glanced in his direction as he passed. He heard them laughing when he drew the blinds.

"Knock, knock. How are you today?" Allie opened the door and stuck her head in. A sense of relief washed over him when he saw her face. He couldn't stop himself from beaming ear to ear. "Hey, Allie, come in and pull up a chair."

"Don't mind if I do. Oh, God, Jamal, what did you do to your face?"

He frowned for a moment, unsure what she meant.

"You changed your beard. It's so much better than it was before."

"Oh, this," he said, stroking his chin. "I figured it was time to give myself a little maintenance."

"It looks gorgeous, Jamal. Very rugged and sexy."

"Wow. No one has ever called my beard sexy before. It's just a tool for modesty."

"Well, don't look so down about it. Some people in this world are just hot. No matter how they try to simmer it down, nothing works. Even with the full beard you had going on before, you were smoking hot," she said, fanning herself with the folder in her hands.

"Thanks," he said, blushing. "My mom always says that she would have pushed me to model if she thought it wouldn't lead to a life of debauchery," he said, flashing his teeth.

"It's never too late," Allie said.

"Are you kidding? Me, a model? I—"

A light knock at the door cut the conversation short.

"Yes?" Jamal asked.

Hannah, the receptionist from the front desk, opened the door. Her eyebrows shot up. "Hey, Jamal, don't you look different? Mister Ashraf would like to see you in the conference room. Allie, this concerns you too, hon."

"Thank you, Hannah," Jamal said.

"No problem. By the way, how's your finger?"

"It's a little better today." He figured she'd want to hear that and not that it hurt like hell. "Allie, we can meet up again after this," Jamal said, rising. "I wonder what this is about; we don't have a meeting on the books, do we?"

Allie checked her phone. "Nope. I don't think everyone is here, anyway."

"There's only one way to find out," Jamal said, ushering Allie out the door.

"WHAT'S THIS MEETING ABOUT? I'm expecting a client soon," Tim asked, checking his watch. There were only five of them in the small room. The four top salespeople and Allie.

"We're here just like you, Tim. We don't know what's going on either," Chauncey said.

"You didn't seem like you were in a hurry ten minutes ago when you were getting the gossip in the break room," Renee said to Tim.

"Yeah, that's because I was killing time. Now, time is killing me," Tim said, sulking in his chair.

"You are such a drama king," Renee said, sipping on an iced coffee. Jamal rolled his eyes. He sat in the only available seat next to her, but it wasn't a complete loss. She crossed her long, brown legs and wiggled her foot, flexing her calves. Renee was a bitch, but she wasn't ugly.

She caught him staring and met his eyes. For once, he didn't look away. He'd never noticed how pretty her eyes were. "Why are you staring at my legs? I thought you only got off on white girls," Renee said.

"I'm not looking at you," Jamal said, blushing.

Renee glared. "You fucking liar. I saw you. Like a dog in heat."

Jamal returned the glare. He hated girls like her, always thinking the world wanted them.

"I have a preference. There's nothing wrong with that," he said.

"Be honest. You couldn't pull a Black woman if you had her tied on a leash," Renee said.

"Jamal, let me help you out, brother," Chauncey said, reaching into his pocket. "Take this," he said, handing Jamal a red and white business card across the table. "Daniel Banks is the man you want to see. He'll hook you up with a sweet fade on your beard, man. I mean, you can do it yourself, which you obviously did, or you can get it professionally done and look less like a chump." Renee and Tim laughed. Jamal's light brown complexion turned a deep shade of red.

"Sorry I'm late, everyone. I was out at the new subdivision, driving across the wretched gravel roads and got a small dent in the side of my car from a loose rock," Saalih said, entering the boardroom.

"Not the Jag? My poor baby," Renee said. Everyone in the room groaned. "What? I love that car. I feel like if something bad happens to it, something bad happens to me too," she said.

"Yeah, you had that dent in your head for as long as I can remember," Tim said. Jamal watched as Saalih laughed with the rest of them. He noticed his boss seemed loose and in good spirits, so the meeting must not be too serious. He checked the time on his phone and hoped it wouldn't take too long, since he had cold calls to make.

"Okay, everyone, settle down. I called this last-minute meeting because a buddy of mine has not one, but two multi-million-dollar condos to move. I want you all to break up into teams and sell these properties. They are smoking hot, and he wants them moved by next week."

"Next week?" Chauncey asked.

"You don't want them for yourself?" Tim asked, suspicious as usual.

"Unfortunately, I will need to take a break over the next couple of weeks. My mother is moving to Virginia to live with my family permanently. I need to collect her from Pakistan and get her settled. When I get back, I will announce which one of you will have earned the corner offices."

"Both corner offices are up for grabs?" Tim asked.

"Yes. Winning team takes all. The top seller amongst the winners gets the bigger office."

"Who is selling what, Mister Ashraf?" Renee asked.

"I'm splitting everyone up. Chauncey and Renee are on one team; Tim, Jamal, and Allie on the other."

Jamal gritted his teeth. His biggest competitor was staring back at him on the other side of the table with a wide grin.

"No offense to Allie, but why did you put her on our team, Ashraf? Not to sound mean, but why is she here at all? She's not a closer," Tim said. Chauncey lifted the brochure up to his face to hide the shock on his face and Renee let out a low groan. Tim knew how to dish out blunt criticism.

"That's okay," Ashraf said, folding his arms. "I understand Jamal has taken Allie under his wing, so he's mentoring her as well as vying for a shot at the office."

Jamal looked across the table from Saalih to Allie. It was supposed to be a one-time thing, not an ongoing mentorship.

"Allie will shadow Jamal and you as well, Tim. Meanwhile, she's got her own houses to move. Isn't that right, Allison?"

"Yes, Sir, that's right."

"Okay, here are the scripts for each property. Decide among yourselves who gets what. They are almost equal in value and are both in pristine condition, hardly lived in by the owners. I'm leaving on a flight this evening. Hannah will contact me if there's an emergency. Do you have any questions?"

No one made a sound except to flip over the printed information about the condos. Jamal scanned the room and saw people putting on their game faces. Allie wasn't interested in the paperwork at all. She was staring at him from across the table and twirling her hair around her finger. Jamal tried to convince himself that she wasn't staring, just spacing out, but the look in her eyes was anything but vacant; it was smoldering and deliberate. Jamal tugged at his shirt collar, irritated. It was hard for him to concentrate on two things at once.

"Alright, meeting over. When I come back, I want to hear good news. I'll be counting your commissions down to the penny for the corner offices. Be well, and let's get out there and make some money."

Everyone stood, buzzing with excitement as Saalih exited the room. "Hold up, hold up," Chauncey said. "Which place do y'all want?"

"Which one do you want, Chauncey?" Tim asked in reply. "We know you like to trick people into taking the opposite, so be honest for once in your life and spill it."

"We want this one," Jamal said, showing them the flier of a modern three-million-dollar condo with a private driveway and a four-car garage.

"Why that one?" Tim asked.

"Because he wants this one," Jamal said.

"Why do you think I want that one?" Chauncey asked.

"Because you keep sliding the paper over to me. You want me to think you're being diplomatic? Chauncey, you can't pay people to buy houses lately. You're going down, big man," Jamal said. Chauncey sat in complete silence, studying Jamal's poker face. Jamal returned the stare.

"Come on, guys. We don't have time for your dick-swinging, I have a client to meet," Tim said, waving papers between them. "Chauncey, decide already. And Jamal, man, chill. It's a friendly competition, right?"

"Yeah, when did you become hard?" Renee asked from behind.

"When he looked at your legs," Chauncey said.

"I wasn't looking at her legs," Jamal insisted.

"Sure, you weren't," Chauncey said. "What are you up to, Jamal? Do you really think you're going to get that corner office? Not while I'm around. Pick one," Chauncey said, holding out the brochures.

Jamal kept his eyes on Chauncey's and reached for one of the property sheets. His hand stopped and drew back from it. He peered at the paper where the contact info should be.

You're going to die for stealing my home.

"What the fuck?"

Chauncey jumped and dropped the papers on the table. "What is it? A spider? I hate spiders, get it away." He slapped at himself, throwing back his chair and bolting to the other side of the room.

Renee picked up the papers. "What is it?" she asked, scanning the papers. "'A property to die for. It's a steal.' I don't see the problem."

Jamal looked at the paper again. "It... it was a spider," he said. "It's gone now."

"I can't believe you and Chauncey are afraid of spiders at your old ages," Renee said.

Jamal grabbed a paper from her hand. "I don't care which one we sell either. When I get my new office, you can make an appointment to come and visit any time you like," Jamal said, handing the property listing to Tim.

"Whatever, man," Chauncey said, picking up his bag and heading for the door. "By the way, Jamal. When Renee and I finish selling ours, you can put yours on my desk, and we'll sell that one too. Lord knows you've got enough on your hands babysitting," he said, nodding towards Allie. "Sorry, Tim, looks like you're on the losing team this time." He turned and strolled out of the office with Renee hot on his heels. She turned back and gave Jamal the finger.

"Don't worry about me, Chauncey. I don't need you to be on my team. We're going to sell The Big House and win this thing."

"The Big House?" Jamal asked.

"It needs a name," Tim shrugged. "Anyway, I'm out of here, Jamal. My uncle flew in from Vancouver and he wants to buy two properties from me. There's no way in hell I'm going to pass that up. So long, suckers," he said, walking out the door.

"And then there were two," Allie said.

"One. I've got to get some cold calling done for this open house."

"When is it?" Allie asked.

"Tomorrow, if I can swing it. I need to call around and line up some buyers."

"Tell you what," Allie said. "I need to be at one of my locations in forty minutes. I have four potential buyers visiting during the next two hours. If you come with me and talk to these people, I'll split the commission with you fifty-fifty and help you with your cold calls."

"Allie—"

"Please, Jamal? Mentor? I need you."

Jamal looked into her green cat eyes and shook his head. He didn't understand why she couldn't talk at least one person into buying the house when she seemed to have such a hold on him. He felt drawn to her, as if she had compelled him with a spell.

"Fine, I'll do it. I hate cold calling anyway," he said.

"Who doesn't? Let me grab my purse and we can go."

CHAPTER TEN

"WHAT HAPPENED TO YOUR FINGER?" Allie sat down in the front passenger seat of the Escalade and adjusted the position of Qaylah's seat to accommodate her long legs. She was a bit shorter than him, which put her around five-foot-ten or eleven.

"I cut it on something," he said.

"It could use a fresh bandage." She reached into her purse. "Does it hurt?"

"Not right now, but the damn thing keeps swelling, even though it looks like it's healing."

"Must be infected. You should take some ibuprofen just in case. Here we are," she said, fishing a bandage out of the bottom of her purse.

"I can't change it while I'm driving," he said.

"Don't worry, I'll do it." Allie reached over and took his hand off the wheel.

"Be careful, Allie," Jamal said, swerving. "It could wait until we arrive at the property, you know."

"Relax. Concentrate on driving and leave the rest to me. You're in excellent hands, so to speak." A mischievous grin crossed her face. Jamal kept still.

"There's a first aid kit in the glove box," he said.

"Good. It smells a little janky. You might try washing it."
Allie laid his hand on her lap and opened the glove compartment. She leaned forward, brushing his fingertips with the underside of her breasts, and the car veered into the other lane. "Steady, Jamal. You wouldn't want to cause an accident."

She grabbed the brand new kit and worked on his finger in silence. Jamal felt hyper aware of the stinging pain brought on by gentle dabs of a cotton ball. He released the breath he was holding and breathed in the fresh scent of her hair and the musky smell of her perfume.

"Do you mind?" she asked, turning on the air conditioning without waiting for a reply. The max setting blew her hair away from her freckled face, exposing the white skin on her neck.

His eyes slipped away from the road and traveled down to the delicate hollow between her shoulder and collarbone for a moment. A throbbing ache passed through his body, lingering between his thighs. He wanted to say something. The words didn't come.

"Where are we headed?" he asked.

"Triton Road. The nearest intersection is Franklin and Jefferson Avenue. The car smells nice," she said.

"Yeah, I ran it through the car wash several times today."

"Why?" she asked.

"Shit happens," he said.

"Bird?"

"Dog," he told her.

She sat up. "A dog pooped on your car?"

"Yup. The little devil rubbed it all over the hood and the roof."

"Oh, God, Jamal. What did you do?"

"What could I do? The neighbor came out of his house and threatened to shoot me if I hurt it. I was already holding the broom when I came outside. I wasn't gonna do anything to it."

"He had some nerve. It would suck to live next door to someone like that."

"He doesn't live next door to me. He's the neighbor next door to the house I'm selling."

"There's nothing you can do about that."

"Not a thing. Unless he brings his gun over. Apparently, he's no stranger to the local law enforcement."

"I hope you sell it fast before the buyers find out who lives there. Turn left here, then one more left." He turned onto Triton Road and took in the neighborhood. The street looked like something out of a brochure.

"Do you like my sign?" The third home on the left had a beautiful black sign out front. He smiled at her but burned with envy. Allie's blazer and pearls made her look more mature and professional than she did in real life. You'd never guess by looking at the sign that she couldn't pay someone to take a house off her hands.

"This is it," she said, following Jamal up the walk. He'd done his homework by reading up on the location's specs online to get an idea of what he was walking into. He couldn't figure out what was keeping her from selling the house.

"As far as I can tell, this place is worth fighting for; so why isn't anyone chasing you down to buy it?" he asked.

"I don't know. I've listed it and called around to announce the showcasing. People resist when I mention it to them. I think I'm the problem."

"Don't give up, Allie. I'm here with you. We're gonna get this place crossed off your list and then do the same thing with the other property."

"If you say so, I believe it," she said.

"Thanks. You're too kind to me."

"I mean it, Jamal. Spending time with you has given me hope. Your willing participation helps further my dreams."

"Okay, now you're just sucking up," he said grinning, "but I dig it. Let's go check out this house before the people get here."

They sat down at a makeshift desk Allie made from a small table. Jamal laid out a runner and poured expensive chocolates wrapped in gold foil into a bowl for the guests to grab. Allie placed feature sheets on the desk with both of their business cards attached.

He watched her from behind while she fretted over the position of a set of throw pillows. Her behind was small but toned. It had him mesmerized. His phone buzzed. Qaylah. He turned off the ringer and Allie set a portable speaker on the table. Smooth jazz filled the space while candles created a sense of atmosphere. It might be romantic if they weren't working.

Jamal reached into a gift bag that he brought in from the car and pulled out the contents.

"A tablet? What's that for? Are you giving it away?"

"Uh huh," he said, propping the box up on a stand at the end of the narrow table. "This is how you reduce or eliminate your cold calls in the future. Everyone should enter their information on these sweepstakes entries for the tablet. We'll call them in a few days."

Allie whipped out her phone to take notes. "What should I say?"

Jamal shrugged. "Thank them for coming out. Find out what they're looking for and tell them you're the one who can give it to them. Chit-chat. Let them do the talking, then feed off of what they tell you. Now, you've become better acquainted. Tell them the draw for names will be at the end of the month."

"Nice. Then I draw names?"

"Nah. Just give it to the first one who calls you before the month is over. Otherwise, save it for the next time."

"Really?"

"Yes. Nobody expects to win these things anyway," Jamal said.

"Out of curiosity, how long have you had that tablet?" She asked.

"Since it came out last year. I never give them away until they're about to become obsolete."

"Sneaky," she said.

"Now, if your clients get into a bidding war, give a tablet to the loser, and find them a home that checks off everything they loved about this one as fast as you can."

"I hope to have that problem," Allie said, smiling.

"Don't worry. It happens all the time, and it's a rush. I've never done drugs, but the feeling I get when I'm swimming in buyers is intoxicating."

Jamal gave the interior of the house a quick once-over as he turned on every light throughout the house. He opened the last bedroom and switched on the light. He yelled before he could stop himself. The woman with the weathered black skin hung from the ceiling, her eyes bulging.

"Jamal, you okay up there?"

He blinked, and what he thought he saw wasn't there after all. "Fine. I hit my finger but I'm alright." He felt like a child running from the boogeyman as he descended the staircase. The atmosphere took a turn from laid back and sexy to creepy as hell. He made it in time to greet four couples at the front door.

"Hello, how are y'all doing today? I'm Jamal Jackson, and this is my colleague, Allie Swanson. Welcome to our open house." He took a deep breath, willing his mind to calm itself.

The potential buyers poured inside and left their shoes at

the door or put the complimentary shoe covers over them. "Please be sure to sign the guest book and pick up an entry form for a chance to win the tablet that you see on the table." They stood in line, awaiting their chances to sign the book.

"Walk around and get a feel for the place," Jamal said. "If you have questions, we'll be right here, waiting to answer them for you."

The couples diverged, exploring different areas of the house while Jamal and Allie waited. An older man returned twice for the chocolates, but Jamal suspected he was using them as an excuse to get a closer look at Allie. He couldn't blame him for that. She looked stunning in the new dress she purchased from the mall.

The man straightened up and walked towards the sliding glass doors that led to the backyard when a woman in orange shorts returned.

"Hi, I'm Mary Lombardi. I was wondering, how long would it take to close on this house?"

"It will take between thirty and forty-five days," Jamal answered.

"Do you have a card?" she asked.

"I sure do," Jamal said, handing her one from the table of spec sheets. "My name is Jamal Jackson, and this is Allie Swanson. You can reach us by phone any time, day, or night."

He answered her questions then ushered in a new group of potential buyers at the front door as she left.

"I've never seen this many people interested in buying this place," Allie said. Her eyes grew wide with excitement. "You're my good luck charm." Allie reached up and pulled his face towards hers, grazing his cheek.

Jamal cleared his throat and leaned away to straighten his tie. "It's not luck. The asking price of this house is a bargain. I mean, look at it. I wish I could buy a house like this for my family."

"I doubt you're suffering," Allie said, leaning on the table behind her. "You are the same guy driving a Cadillac, right?"

"Yes," he nodded. "I am the same guy driving a Cadillac. My dad's old car. He sold it to me for pennies or I'd never be able to afford it. I'm a regular guy receiving nine-to-five pay for twelve-hour shifts."

The ringing cellphone on the table interrupted their conversation, but Allie didn't make a move to answer it.

"Aren't you gonna get that?"

"It's my work phone," Allie said.

"Okay, all the more reason to pick up."

Allie brought her hands to her face. "What if it's a buyer?"

"Yes, Allie. What if it is? Look at it, Allie. See who it is."

She dropped her hands and answered the phone. "It's the woman in the orange shorts from the open house."

"Already? She can't have gotten far," Jamal said.

Allie tossed the phone on the table and turned away from it. "I can't do it, Jamal. I'll screw it up."

"No, you won't, Allie. All you need to do is let the customer tell you what they want. If you can deliver, say yes. If you can't, tell them what you can do for them and let them decide, or give them another option."

Allie shook her head, and he watched the fear diminish as she reached for the phone. She smiled, crooked and unsure, and crossed her fingers.

～

"Oh my God, Jamal, you are the man. We should go out and celebrate." Jamal watched Allie pump her fist in the air a second, then a third time. He found the short bursts of happiness endearing.

They sat in the office, filling out paperwork for the potential sale of the property to Miss Mary Lombardi. Jamal got on the phone and convinced Miss Lombardi that the house would go fast in the current market. Based on the huge turnout for the open house, she believed him.

"Miss Lombardi, can you hear that? My office phones are ringing off the hook with people anxious about the sale of this house. Yes, the same property that you're asking for. Hold on a moment, I need to answer the line. The receptionist is getting swamped." Before Jamal put her on hold, he let her listen to the phones ring.

What Jamal didn't mention was Allie sitting in the chair next to him, dialing the office phones and hanging up.

"She's got it bad for this property but doesn't want to admit it," Jamal said.

"You're the one who's bad," Allie said.

"I know," he said, picking up the line. "Thank you for holding, Miss Lombardi." Allie offered him a mischievous smile and dialed his office phone again.

CHAPTER ELEVEN

"QAYLAH, I'M HOME." Jamal tossed his keys towards the rickety entryway table and kicked off his shoes. "Ow, shit."

His keyring caught on his bad finger and fell to the floor. He clamped his other hand over his mouth, hoping Qaylah hadn't heard him swearing. He didn't need an argument to ruin his high.

Speaking with Miss Lombardi had been a fruitful endeavor. By the end of the phone call, he had convinced her that she should sign off on the house before someone else came along and snagged it.

It wasn't much of an exaggeration; when the call ended, other potential buyers from the open house called to make offers on the home. Jamal disclosed he was representing Miss Lombardi, but none of them took their offers off the table. It was rare, but the three interested parties, including Miss Lombardi, insisted on competing for the house. All three of them scheduled a time to offer a bid to the seller. This property was going to move fast.

"Qaylah, wait until you hear about what happened today," he said, searching through empty rooms. "Qaylah, where are you, baby?" His optimism had him flying high.

"She's asleep." Katie stood at the top of the stairs, eyeing Jamal with Mister Sniffles lodged in the crook of her arm.

"Why are you awake, Jellybean?"

"The lady was telling me a story."

"What lady, Katie?"

"The one you talk to at night."

"How many times do I have to tell you that I haven't been talking to anyone at night?" The lady is a figment of your imagination."

"Nah uh. I saw you in the kitchen with her. She was sucking on your finger. But how did she get up there on that rope? Doesn't it hurt her neck?"

Ice ran through Jamal's veins. "What did you say?"

"The lady says she wants to get her house back for her family. She says she's gonna bother us until you give her what she wants."

Jamal shook his head. Sometimes Katie was downright weird, but this seemed beyond the scope of her three-year-old imagination. He hadn't spent much time around young children, even though his siblings had kids. He'd never cared about any of his nieces and nephews on more than a superficial level, not even bothering to learn the spellings of their names.

He hadn't been spending time with her like he wanted. She must have cooked up the story about the lady to cope with his absence. But how did she know about his hallucinations with the woman swinging from the rope? Had he fallen asleep in front of the television one night with Katie at his side?

Either way, she'd have to make do until he sold this house. Then she'd have all the attention she could handle. "Katie, you, and Mister Sniffles have to get back to bed. I've had a long night and I need to eat some dinner. Right now, I'm hungry for little girls. Have you seen any?" Jamal growled like a bear.

Katie's face lit up and a sly grin spread across her tiny

mouth. "You can't catch me, Jamal." She screeched and took off towards her bedroom.

"Here I come, Katie. I'm coming to get you!" The corners of his mouth turned upwards at the sight of the bouncing coils of thick red hair. They reminded Jamal of mattress springs. He scanned the darkness, searching for the little girl.

"Katie? Where are you hiding, Jellybean? Are you under here?" He snatched the covers off the bed, surprised by the lumpy, human-shaped pillow. Shadows and shapes morphed into tangible objects as his eyesight adjusted in the dim room.

Jamal used his bear growl, attempting to rouse the child out of her hiding spot. "I'm here, Katie. I can see you... Aha!" He threw back the bed skirt and poked his head underneath the metal frame. Where was she? Of course. He felt dumb not looking in the most obvious hiding place. He rose and headed to the closet, swinging open the doors. Nope.

"Katie?" A bump on his foot drew his attention to the carpet. A red ball came to an abrupt stop. Jamal bent down and scooped it off the floor. It was an ancient stress ball he had brought home from the office when he first started. The old version of the Ashraf Realty logo had partially scratched off.

"How did you sneak out without me noticing?" He squeezed the ball in his good hand, crushing the air from it until he felt the dry, crumbly texture of the polyurethane. "Okay, Jellybean. I think you should come back to your room and go to bed. It's late."

He released the ball and tossed it into a pile of toys in the corner. Jamal sighed and noticed for the first time that he could see his breath in the moonlight shining through the curtained window. It was colder here than in the rest of the house. The place was temperamental, and thanks to outdated windows and a raggedy roof, the house heated up with the seasons and froze during snowstorms. It was nearing summer; even the surrounding mountainous region was warm enough at night to sleep without a heater. Why was the air so cold? He considered starting a fire in the old wood stove in the kitchen, even though Qaylah warned him not to leave it unattended.

"Come on, Katherine. Let's get to bed." Silence. Using Katie's full name worked for Qaylah, but Jamal sounded stiff and unconvincing. Katie must have agreed. Not a peep or a giggle came out of her.

His teeth chattered in the dark hallway. He didn't remember the lights being out before. He flipped the switch and turned it on. At the far end of the hall, the master bedroom door shut. Qaylah refused to close it unless they were intimate. *Gotcha.*

"You're not sleeping between me and your mom, Katie. Come here." Jamal stepped under the dome light in the hallway, and the light turned off again. "Shit." Plunged into darkness, something shot past him, brushing his arm as it went. He spun around and reached out, half-expecting to grab the little girl by the hair.

He walked towards his room and flicked the other switch at the opposite end of the wall. Darkness. "Damn this place." His irritation bubbled beneath the surface. The landlord was one of the worst he had seen, refusing to fix anything, no matter how urgent, and most of it was beyond Jamal's scope of handiness.

The longer this took, the more drained he felt. It didn't matter whether the light came on or not. It could wait until morning, after a good night's sleep. Jamal peered into Katie's dark room. The night light on the far wall in the little girl's room flickered to life. The bed was empty. *Find Katie first, then sleep.*

Jamal's ears perked up at the sound of her giggles. An immediate release of tension spread from the corners of his mouth into a full grin. Laughter from a child is a beautiful thing.

His heart softened. Katie would be a big sister to his son in a few months. When he was old enough, he could join in and play hide-and-seek with them. Qaylah hated his assumption that their baby was a boy, but he knew it in his heart.

At last, Katie stepped into the doorway. The silly grin on her lips opened into a wide circle as sleepiness caught up with her. Jamal approached the little girl and looked down at her innocent face.

"Time to sleep, Katie. You're getting good at hiding from me. I'm impressed that you can sneak around so fast." Katie drew her arms upwards, beckoning him to carry her to bed. He heard a commotion at the front of the house. Jamal snapped his head towards the door. He side-stepped Katie and peered over the second-floor railing as it opened. Qaylah stepped inside with Katie trailing behind her.

"Katie?" Dumbfounded, he stepped back from the rail. His mind raced to formulate an explanation but faltered. *How is this possible?* An oppressive, heavy feeling over his shoulder left him reluctant to turn towards the bedroom. In the end, he had to know. Curiosity won and he twisted his neck and saw her.

Jamal's eyes bulged as a woman with an unusually long, black arm grasped him by the throat. Before her fingers dug into him, cutting off his airway, the distinct smell of decay filled his nostrils. She stood two heads shorter than him, but her grip was ironclad, dropping him to his knees.

Jamal looked up at her through the slits of his eyelids, as he beat at her forearm with his fists. The effort left him even more depleted of oxygen and closer to panic. He leaned backwards to throw her off balance, but the woman's grip tightened, pulling him back to an awkward sitting position.

"As Salaamu Alaikum, Jamal, we're home." He heard

Qaylah moving downstairs, turning on lights in the kitchen and living room, oblivious to the scuffle on the second floor.

"Maybe he's not here yet." Katie's voice carried as she turned on the television. She sat within the scope of Jamal's peripheral vision on the sofa. Jamal flailed his arms but went unnoticed. If he knew his stepdaughter, her eyes were glued to her favorite evening cartoons. Katie wouldn't have seen him unless he were in front of the t.v.

The hallway light came on, and Jamal saw the woman's face. Her eyes, set deep inside the sockets, studied him. The jet-black skin on her hand felt cold. Dead. It contrasted with the bright red dress she wore.

"He has to be here, Katie. His car is outside," Qaylah said, standing in the living room next to the sofa. "I'll check upstairs, then warm up our dinner."

"Okay," Katie said. Jamal's vision turned yellow with black spots. He had to do something now or risk losing consciousness. He reached out a shaky hand, grabbing at a baluster on the railing. The tips of his fingers slipped, moistening the wood with streaks of sweat. The woman's grip threatened to tear through the tendons and bones in his neck. "Qaylah. Qaylah..." He mouthed her name, but no sound escaped.

The woman leaned into his face and blew hot air into his mouth. Although he couldn't smell it, he began to retch. "I want my fucking house back. Get it for me or I'll kill your family before I kill you." Jamal crashed to the hardwood floor, and the world went black.

"Oh, my God. Jamal. Jamal!" The slapping sound of Qaylah's feet on hardwood stairs stopped beside his ears. He heard the swish of her abaya as she leaned down and checked his pulse. She roused him, giving his shoulders a hard shake. "Jamal, honey. Wake up."

Oxygen returned to his body in one painful breath, and he

lifted his arm off the floor at the elbow, gripping her shoulder. "Qaylah."

"Alhamdulillah. Thank God," she said, burying her face in his chest. "I thought I lost you." She sat up and looked down at him. "Can you sit up?"

Jamal squinted at her head, haloed by the ceiling light. He sat up and leaned against the railing. "I saw her."

Qaylah helped him off the floor. "Who? Who did you see, Jamal?"

"I saw the dead woman. She wants her house back."

A gasp prompted them to look towards the stairs. Katie was standing at the top, clutching Mister Sniffles, and an old stress ball.

"DO YOU HEAR THAT TAPPING?" Jamal studied the wall behind the stove. Qaylah had served burnt pancakes and eggs for breakfast. The eggs had bits of shells in them, but no one complained.

"No, Jamal. It's your imagination. Can't we eat in peace?" Her voice sounded strained.

"You haven't touched your food," he said.

"I'm not hungry." Qaylah pushed away from the table and took her plate to the sink.

Jamal looked across the table at Katie. She stopped poking at her pancakes and met Jamal's eyes. He shuddered and looked away.

Maybe Qaylah was right. Maybe he passed out, and the woman had been a figment of his imagination. "What about Katie? Was that my imagination too?"

"I think that's obvious, since she was with me," Qaylah whispered. She hated discussing adult things with Katie around. Jamal wouldn't drop it. Couldn't drop it until he figured out what had happened to him last night.

"I can't believe you would blame my daughter for your condition. She didn't hurt you."

"I didn't say she hurt me. I said the woman, or whatever I saw, looked like Katie at first. Then *she* hurt me."

"That sounds an awful lot like you're saying Katie hurt you."

"No, it doesn't. You're being defensive."

"And you're being silly. No one was in the house. You saw for yourself. And why the heck would somebody want to break into this dump? It's eighty years old and falling apart."

"How should I know? I have no desire to spend my life in this house."

"At least we agree." Qaylah walked to the table and whispered in his ear. "I don't want Katie hearing this conversation. She seems spooked."

"She doesn't look spooked."

"Jamal," Qaylah said.

"But this is important."

"I think you were having a dream, Jamal. Sometimes the brain concocts hallucinations to get our attention when something is wrong. For whatever reason, you passed out and your mind tried its best to rouse you from sleep. Don't forget to pray. It'll make you feel better," she said, kissing his cheek.

The conversation changed after that. "Are you alright, Qaylah? I think you should eat something. You look frail."

"I don't feel like eating. The nausea is getting intense."

"I'm sorry to hear that," he said, checking the time. Jamal slid his chair from under the table and stood. "I have to go to work. Thanks for breakfast."

"Thanks for wasting my time and not eating it," she said. He gave her a kiss and walked to the front door.

"You didn't say goodbye to Katie," Qaylah said, trailing after him.

He reached out and ran a finger down her cheek. "Have you ever considered dying your hair red?"

"What?"

"Never mind," he said, slipping on his shoes. "Tell her I said goodbye. I've got to go." Jamal walked out the door and climbed into his Cadillac. He ignored his wife's face, peering out from behind the curtain.

He massaged his temples and thought about last night. *My brain was trying to wake me, she says.* Qaylah didn't believe him. She thought the entire ordeal was an exaggeration or hallucination because he fainted. Jamal pulled back the folds of his collar and studied his throat in the mirror. The four dark red half-moons on his neck raised questions he couldn't answer. But they were certainly not his imagination.

CHAPTER TWELVE

JAMAL ENTERED his office and took the laptop out of his messenger bag before tossing it onto the floor next to his desk. He sat down in his chair, then turned on the computer. After skimming a few emails, he got up and walked to the break room.

"What's going on, Tim?"

"Not much, man. Did you get your name on the board yet?" Tim Chang was third in line for home sales, although his expertise was moving commercial properties. In the past year, Tim's family had made a mass exodus from British Columbia to Rosewood Hollow, sending his sales through the roof in both endeavors. Jamal had his eyes on him.

"No, not yet. I've got this stubborn house on Spiegel Road that I'm selling. There are a couple other ones I'm working on too."

"Yeah, I heard you were working with Allie. Or, are you working *in* Allie?" Tim raised an eyebrow and laughed. He poured the last of the coffee into his mug and left the empty pot on the burner without rinsing it out and brewing a new batch. It figures. Renee complained about the mess in the break room all day. Mystery solved.

"I've been mentoring her," Jamal said.

Tim laughed and took a long sip of his coffee. "Good on you for working her sales. Make sure you get half, even though you'll be doing all the work. That girl's a flake. I'd bang her though."

Jamal rubbed the side of his neck and winced.

"Are you alright?" Tim asked, pointing to Jamal's hand. The cut on his finger was bleeding again, soaking through the bandage.

"Yeah. I cut it on something. It keeps bleeding."

"You better get it checked out. I have a cousin who cut her finger and ended up in a coma for three weeks. Turned out to be a staph infection."

Jamal turned on his bullshit meter. Tim had a cousin story about every type of calamity on earth. "You drank the last of the coffee. Renee's gonna bitch about it."

"Man, when doesn't Renee bitch. Do you want to make some more? I could use another cup. I've got to keep my energy up for the rest of the morning. My aunties are bugging me about a couple of houses in Edgewater."

"Edgewater?" The luxurious gated community of Edgewater was in the far west end of Rosewood Hollow. There was no such thing as poor housewives in that neck of the woods. Husbands and wives had matching high-interest bank accounts there. Cinderella had to look elsewhere for a spouse. Housewife or not, you came with your own money, or you didn't belong.

"You know how it is," Tim said. "You're not still living in that house on Ayer Road, are you?" Tim looked up everyone's address to compare it to his. Jamal didn't fault him for it—they all did it, but they didn't broadcast it to the whole damn world like Tim did.

"I'm still there. I'm saving up to buy a home soon."

"You're serious? You can't buy a house on a mortgage because your sky daddy said it's forbidden?"

Jamal clenched his teeth and shoved a spoon into the packed coffee grinds. "Tim, I'd appreciate it if you wouldn't disrespect me in the workplace."

Tim's eyebrows raised, and he held his hands up in surrender. "Hey, man, I'm just saying. It seems to me you're creating unnecessary hardships in your life with all these archaic rules and regulations." Tim ran his fingers through his hair. He had one of those afro perms and a fade like Jamal had seen on TikTok. Renee went after him for appropriation until he went after her for wearing blonde wigs and blue contacts.

"We all believe in something," Jamal said, turning on the brewer.

"You're right," Tim said. "My god is money. It tells me where I can go, what I can do, and how many hot girls I can bring along for the ride." Tim held his empty mug under the stream of coffee in the brewer and refilled his mug.

"Hey, what are y'all talking about?" Chauncey entered the break room and opened the fridge. He perused the food items like he was at home.

Renee came in, hot on his heels, shuffling a deck of black and gold tarot cards. She made herself comfortable at a little table and started laying down the cards. The red dress she wore contrasted with her dark skin. The color made Jamal uncomfortable.

"Don't do that, Tim. You'll get coffee everywhere, but thank you for making a fresh pot, boo. I don't know who keeps leaving it empty, but they are getting on my last nerve. I'm gonna put a little hex on whoever it is," Renee said, rolling her eyes at Jamal.

"Sorry, Renee, I know you hate that," Tim said, pouring

the coffee into his mug the way normal people did. "Jamal and I were talking about who or what we worship."

"Oh, Lord," Renee said.

"No pun intended," Chauncey said, opening a can of orange soda with the name 'Bruce' written on it.

"Are you trying to convert Tim?" Renee asked Jamal.

"What? Why would I do that?" Jamal asked. Something about her rubbed him the wrong way. If Renee had a problem, she'd break her neck to prove that Jamal was the root cause.

"Relax, he doesn't even pray like he used to," Chauncey said, looking at Jamal. "You know, player, you don't have to walk around looking like a runaway slave. I told you before, there are Black barbers in town who can hook up your hair and your beard."

Renee threw her head back and laughed. Jamal hadn't noticed the intricate tattoos on her throat before. She straightened up before he could make out what they were.

"Stop laughing, Renee. It's obvious our brother is in need."

"He's no brother of mine. If he could, he'd be as white as his wife."

"Knock it off, Renee. Jamal, I'll give you my boy's number so he can get you looking clean," Chauncey said, shuffling a handful of business cards. "Here you go, man. Allah likes beauty, homie. Treat yourself." He slapped the card into Jamal's hand and left the room.

"You've got to admit," Tim said, emptying the coffee pot when Renee turned her attention to her cards, "Chauncey's hair is always on point."

❧

"WHO DOES that sonofabitch think he is?" Jamal threw the business card into the sea of papers on his desk. He hated them. Chauncey, Tim, and that scheming bimbo, Renee.

He would shut them up by closing as many houses as he could before the competition ended. Then he'd set up his own coffee station in his beautiful corner office and never go back to that damn break room.

"Knock, knock." Allie closed his office door with her foot and hobbled to his desk balancing two extra-large cups of coffee and a box of donuts from the popular local chain, Sticky Fingers. Another knock sounded at the door.

"You're popular today," Allie said.

"Come in." A tall Black man wearing a gray suit and matching kufi opened the door. Jamal recognized him from the law firm in the plaza. "As Salaamu Alaikum."

"Wa Alaikum As Salaam. Brother, we're about to pray next door. I came to remind you."

Jamal squirmed and scratched the top of his head. His stomach flip-flopped as the recent memory of his sickness at the masjid rose to the surface. "Thanks." The man nodded and waited in the doorway. "You can go on without me. I'll be over in a minute, brother."

"Time's running out. We aren't usually this late, but we had an important client."

"Then start without me and I'll either come over or pray in my office."

The man glanced at Allie then back to Jamal and nodded. "Salaam." The door closed and Jamal exhaled slowly. The sick feeling left him and his appetite returned. He reached for the donut box.

"Thanks for thinking of me." There were two camps of donut lovers in the Tri-Cities: those who loved Sticky Fingers and those who would camp out over the weekend to get fresh donuts from Josephine's Bakery and Jazz Café. Jamal felt like a traitor as he lifted a dry-looking glazed donut from the box.

"You're welcome. I never pegged you for a plain donut kind of guy. You seem more exciting than that," Allie said, flopping down in a chair.

"Glazed donuts need love too," he said, biting down on the gummy pastry. He worked it in his mouth, swallowing chunks of the dense dough until it became apparent that he needed a swig of coffee to swallow it.

Allie clapped her hands and threw her head back in a fit of laughter, exposing the slender line of her neck. "You don't like it, do you?"

Jamal took his time clearing his mouth with the mediocre coffee. "Have you been to Josephine's?"

"What's that?" She asked, wiping tears from the corners of her eyes with a napkin.

"Get your stuff. We're gonna work outside."

"Shouldn't you go pray first?"

"I'll make it up later." Jamal grabbed his car keys, careful not to disturb his throbbing finger.

CHAPTER THIRTEEN

"Mmm, oh my God. Jamal, these are amazing." Allie licked her fingers, getting every bit of the cream she spilled from her donut.

Jamal smiled, proud of himself for introducing her to one of his guilty pleasures. "I told you they were good."

"Good doesn't describe this donut. It's... orgasmic."

Jamal looked at the tables to his immediate left and right, wondering if anyone in earshot heard her. "I wouldn't go that far," he said, hiding his sheepish grin behind his coffee cup. He loved how open she was. Qaylah would never say something like that.

"Did I embarrass you?"

"No. A little. We have a lot of work to do. We need those client consent forms if we're going to represent all three buyers."

"I'm on top of it. One of them will arrive at the office in the late afternoon. The others will stop by this evening after work. Hannah set them up with different appointment slots, so they don't run into each other."

"Good."

"What did you have in mind for this morning?" His eyes trailed her tongue as she licked the chocolate off an éclair. Jamal undid a button on his shirt and wiped the sweat from his brow with a napkin. He had a lot on his mind, but none of it was work related.

Their eyes met, and he cleared his throat. "We could run through a couple of foreplay scenarios to help you work on negotiations."

"What did you say?"

"I said role-play."

"You did not."

He wrinkled his forehead. "Didn't I?"

"Nope. You said, 'foreplay.'" Allie's lips were tucked into her mouth.

He closed his eyes. "Oh, God. I feel like an idiot."

"Well, mister mind-in-the-gutter, we'll chalk it up to the sugar," she said. A sly grin broke out on her lips.

"I'm really sorry."

"Don't be. I'm flattered. So, you were saying? Role-play?"

"Yes. Role-play scenarios. You can be the real estate agent and I'll be the customer."

"Boring."

"How so?"

"I'm not in the mood to do that. I'm a visual learner. How about I watch you work?"

"You'd rather watch me work? I have a ton of boring desk work to do. In fact, I'm planning to drop by the house and make sure everything is alright, then I'm going to put in a couple of hours cold-calling and posting listings online."

"How about showing me this house on Spiegel really quick? After that, I'll help you cold call from the office until my clients show up."

"You drive a hard bargain, Allie Swanson."

"It's the least I can do for donuts as tasty as these."

~

Jamal pulled into the driveway at Spiegel an hour later.

"This is a cute little place, Jamal. I can't believe you haven't moved it." Allie unfastened her seatbelt and climbed out of the Escalade. The irony of her statement wasn't lost on him. Jamal followed her as she admired the painted porch and the fresh trim of the hedges.

For a fleeting moment, he pretended Allie was Qaylah, and he was showing her their new house. Their forever home. "I love the curb appeal," Allie said, inspecting the flowers and the large willow trees on the lawn. She stepped to the larger one and rubbed the trunk. "How cute is this? There are initials carved into it. How romantic."

Jamal strolled to the willow to see them. There were several clumsy attempts at carving hearts and initials all over the bark. Allie rested her hand against it and closed her eyes.

"When I was a little girl, my grandmother said you could hear the heart beating inside the trees. The loudest ones tell you where you're supposed to settle down and live. She called it your forever home."

"I kind of like that," Jamal said, placing his palm on the tree. "What if there aren't trees on your land?"

Allie paused for a moment, then opened her eyes. "If there aren't trees, how would you know it belongs to you?"

Jamal studied her face and smiled. "Good question. I guess you'd have to plant them."

"Do you feel anything, Jamal? Do you feel the heart beating?"

Jamal repositioned his hand and closed his eyes. "It just feels like a plain old tree to me."

"Then you're trespassing."

His eyes opened as a blur of black fur zoomed across the yard.

"What the—get off of me. Jamal, help me!" Allie bent down to clutch her calf. "That little fucker bit me." She straightened up and reared back her leg, aiming it at the dog.

"Whoa, whoa, whoa, what the hell do you think you're doing? Don't you dare kick my dog. What's wrong with you, stupid tramp?" Tobias shambled across the yard and picked up Buck.

"Your fucking mutt bit my leg," Allie said, turning to show him the bite mark.

"You can't prove it," Tobias said, running his hands through the thin white tufts of hair on his head. Jamal noticed it matched the ones growing out of his nostrils.

"I have a witness, you idiot."

"He's gonna lie for you. He hates Buck. What are the two of you doing here, anyway? Did you bring her here to screw?"

"Does he have his shots?" Allie jerked her thumb at Buck.

"What do you think, you dumb whore?" Tobias sneered.

"I think I'm calling the police and my attorney."

"Good luck with that, sister. I don't own a damn thing, including that house."

"And I think I'm calling animal control to put him down."

"You wouldn't dare."

"Try me, prick."

Tobias turned to Jamal, terror in his eyes. He wiped the drip from his lips on his sleeve and reached for him. Jamal stepped back. "Say, Mister Jackson, don't let her do that, okay? He's all I've got."

Jamal sighed and looked away. "I'm Mister Jackson today and boy tomorrow. Isn't that right, mister ex-military?"

"I was wrong to disrespect you like that. I had too much to drink."

"Cry me a river," Allie said. The men watched her stick out her leg to get a better angle. She snapped photos of the bite. "You're going down, Tobias. And your little dog, too."

Jamal smiled and looked away. She was angry and corny, but he liked her.

"Has he had his shots or not, grandpa?" Allie took a picture of Tobias and Buck.

"Yes. Yes, he's had them. I keep all his paperwork from the vet. I can show you. He's my pride and joy," Tobias said.

"I feel sorry for you," Allie said, looking up at him.

"Are you telling the truth?" Jamal asked. "Have you been keeping up with his shots?"

Tobias perked up. "Yes. I took him to the vet two, no, three months ago. I can get the papers."

"That won't be necessary, will it? Allie?"

Allie shot a hard glance at Jamal. "He bit me."

"But it didn't break the skin. I have a first aid kit in the car. I can give you some antiseptic to clean the area," Jamal said.

"He's right. I don't think you have anything to worry about if the skin is intact," Tobias said.

"Shut up. No one's talking to you." Allie smoothed her red hair and looked into Jamal's eyes. "Oh, alright," she said, shrugging. "Take your damn mangy dog and get the hell out of here. If I see him off-leash again, I'm calling animal control to come and get him."

"Yes, Ma'am. Thank you," Tobias said, clutching the dog to his chest. Buck barked at Jamal and Allie. "Buck, shut the hell up. Sorry for that, Mister Jackson, Miss Allie." Tobias clutched the dog and retraced his steps out of the yard.

"Let's get you inside to wash that bite," Jamal said, holding his hand out to assist her.

Allie refused it. "Thanks, but I'll be alright. That guy is an idiot. Stupid dog. That's the kind of animal only its owner could love. And maybe my brothers. I'll never understand their love for dogs. I'm a cat person myself."

"I need to get the antiseptic."

"Don't bother. I was just fucking with him." Taken aback, Jamal watched Allie walk up the porch steps. He was seeing a side of her that wasn't so desperate or meek. And he liked it.

JAMAL SET up his computer at the folding table he used for open houses and added listings to his social media pages while Allie explored the upstairs. He heard her opening and closing doors as she moved from room to room.

"I love this place, Jamal. Do you have a buyer yet?"

"No. I can give you a great deal on it if you want to take it off my hands."

"I wish I could," she said, coming down the stairs. "I don't have the money to buy my house yet, and my job status is a little shaky at the moment."

"Don't worry about the job. I'm your mentor, remember?"

"Okay, then I need to come up with about ten to fifteen thousand dollars. Can you mentor me on how to do that?"

"Sell houses. I won't pretend it's gonna be easy though. I'm in the same boat—maybe worse."

"You're trying to buy a home?"

"Yes. My wife is pregnant, and we live in a two-bedroom bungalow with my stepdaughter. The place is a dump, and I swear it's haunted. I'm doing the best I can to come up with enough cash to buy a house outright, but it's going to take a long time."

"Cash? Do you mean you want to buy the house for cash, or save enough for the down payment?"

"The whole shebang. I know it sounds insane, but it's doable with the right investments, the right job—"

"A million years of saving."

"Something like that."

"May I ask why you're doing it that way?"

"Mortgages are forbidden in my religion."

Allie wrinkled her brow. "But you deal with mortgages every day."

"I'm not perfect," Jamal said. He waited for her to pick him apart, to tell him how stupid that sounded to her and that he was wasting his time, like most people did when he had this conversation.

Allie sat down on the other chair and said nothing for a while. "I think it's admirable that you would try this hard to get something you want, even with the odds stacked against you. Don't let people try to discourage you. Most of those naysayers are internalizing your goals and advising you based on their own failures."

"Thank you, Allie. That means a lot. It sounds to me like you're speaking from experience."

She nodded. "Maybe. I too have a healthy fear of debt. People keep telling me how to do my job, but none of them are giving me any real advice. Except you. I know my numbers are low and it seems like I'm on my way out, but I don't think I am."

"You're not. You need to get that commission, then it will be smooth sailing."

"That's not what Tim and Chauncey told me."

"What did they say?"

"The strip club on Paradise Avenue is hiring."

"I'm guessing that came out of Tim's mouth."

"You would be right."

"Are you going to take it up with Ashraf when he comes back?"

"No."

"Why not? It's sexual harassment."

"I'd rather make those guys hurt where it counts."

"Where's that?"

"Their egos. Win the other office," she said. With a crooked smile, Allie held up her hand for a hi-five.

"That's my girl," Jamal said, slapping her palm. Corny, but endearing.

"Hmm," she said.

"What?"

She leaned forward in her chair and lay her hand on his cheek. The intimate contact with her palm made him jerk, then sit upright. He couldn't breathe as she curled her fingers into the wave-pattern of the longer hairs growing near his chin.

"It's soft and it grows so fast. I don't know why Chauncey makes fun of it. Where I come from, all the men of a certain age have beards. I don't mind them, but I'm a sucker for a smooth-faced guy too," she said.

Jamal's mouth went dry. "I think we should get back to work."

"Maybe we should do what you suggested when we were at Josephine's," she said, stroking his face.

"What was that?" He felt his eagerness grow tight in his jeans as she continued to stroke his beard.

"Role-play." The chain strap on Allie's purse vibrated on the table. She let go of Jamal's beard and opened the bag to search for her phone.

"Hello? Yes, this is Allie."

Jamal stood and walked to the kitchen, fighting against the strain in his pants. The cold water shocked him back to life, returning his senses. He took a deep breath and counted his blessings. Whoever was on the phone saved his skin in more ways than one.

He turned off the tap and grabbed a couple of paper towels. He had to get Allie out of the house. Her presence compromised his work and his marriage. Jamal racked his brain for an excuse, but she came into the kitchen before he could plan something solid.

"Hey, I have to go back to the office. The third client wants to meet now instead of this evening. Can you take me back? I'm sorry. I know you wanted to get started on cold calls."

"No, it's fine. I'll take you back right away."

"I'll get my things." Allie spun on her heels and walked to the living room.

Jamal let out a sigh of relief.

CHAPTER FOURTEEN

RELIEF WASHED over Jamal when he came home and found the house dark and empty. He had spent the afternoon putting out fires and calming Allie when two of the buyers dropped out of the bid and the third didn't return her calls. The need to protect her from despair was overbearing when he saw the panic in her eyes.

"Allie, listen to me. People drop out all the time. I've had buyers walk away with the closing papers in their hands. It happens. Don't cry, Allie. Please, don't."

She clung to him in his office for a minute or two, shuddering and crying silent tears. "I'm gonna get fired, I know it."

"Don't talk like that, Allie. You're not getting fired."

"Jamal, I know you're trying to help, but it's no use. I can't sell this house. I'm trying so hard, but it's like I'm cursed."

"Allie, nobody is cursing you. This is real life, and sometimes we fall, but we dust ourselves off and push forward. Let's dig into these call lists and get someone on the phone who wants to buy a house."

She sniffled and wiped the tears from her eyes, then leaned her head into the hollow of his chest. He stared at the perfect strands of red hair protruding from her scalp.

Holding her made his body ache. Jamal felt vulnerable and

unsure of what to do next. It used to feel this way with Qaylah. He shook his head, chasing away thoughts of his wife.

"Damn it, you're right," she said, lifting her head. "I'm feeling better now," Allie said, blowing her nose into a tissue. She fiddled with a bracelet on her arm with various star and moon charms. His fingers rubbed the puffy crescent-shaped scabs on the side of his neck. "Let's do this. Let's find a seller."

"Now you're talking," he said.

They worked into the evening, calling random people on the phone. Later, they switched to client-recommended families, and worked from surveys and sweepstakes entries. Jamal didn't hold back, taking a more aggressive approach than normal.

Today, he was doing double duty by setting up viewings for both of Allie's homes and his one. The good news was that he had arranged a showing for Spiegel Drive tomorrow morning. He expected the young couple, who were parents of two small children, to be serious contenders for the house.

The husband, Asad al-Fihri, was a friend of his from high school. Jamal would give them a gentle push to buy the house. A pang of guilt reminded him they would be living next to Tobias.

"That's great, thank you," Allie said into her phone. She winked her green eyes at him and gave him a thumbs up. Jamal smiled and returned it, feeling like a fool, but not caring.

He ran his fingers through the scruff of his beard. A thought crossed his mind, and he slid a stack of papers out of the way. "Where is it?" he muttered, shuffling papers on his desk. "Ah, there it is." Jamal picked up the discarded business card for the Fade to Black Barber Shop. He turned it over in his hands, studying the logo and phone number.

He'd been growing his beard since he was fourteen years

old. Going without it would make him feel naked. Nobody would recognize him.

"I'm booked solid for the whole day," Allie said.

"That's great news. I'm happy for you. Who gave you your leads?"

"They're from Tim and Renee's old lists. Why?"

"I think they did you dirty, giving you their outdated and picked over numbers." Jamal stood and walked to the small sofa where she camped, with her laptop and a clipboard.

"Their loss," she said.

"Here, take some of these," he said, handing her a couple of sheets. "These are fresh leads that you can call. If you arrange showings, we can work together and split the commissions, okay?"

"Sounds like a deal. Thank you, Jamal."

"You're welcome." She grabbed his hand and held it, caressing it with her thumb. "Sorry about the cold hands," he said. "It's funny. Lately, everywhere I go to feels cold. At home, it feels like I live at the north pole."

"How come you're feeling so cold? Are you coming down with something?"

"I don't know. It's not even the entire house. Just random areas. In some rooms, I can see my breath."

"You have ghosts," she said.

"I don't believe in ghosts."

"Every culture has ghosts. Call them what you want. You've got them."

"We call them jinn."

"They're not exclusive to Muslims. Anyone can be haunted."

"You're right. Their pestering is universal."

"Those cold spots in your house are from spirits."

"I don't think so. Jinn wouldn't enter my house. My wife

reads enough Qur'an and spends a lot of her time praying." When she wasn't cooking or talking about the baby, she was praying or immersing herself in Islamic lectures. Sometimes he wondered if there was anything else to her personality besides her new faith.

"What about your wife?" Allie said with an eyebrow raised.

"What about her?" Jamal asked.

"Does your wife complain about the cold spots?"

"I don't know. The last few weeks have been hectic. I don't think we've been home at the same time in a while." Jamal thought back to the times he noticed the cold.

"Do you read and pray too?" Allie blew into her hands and rubbed them together to warm him.

"Not like I should," he said, giving her a sheepish grin.

"I'm not judging. I sure don't pray like I used to," she said, hooking her finger through a button loop on his shirt. "Have you heard the saying, 'An angel in the streets, a devil in the sheets?'" Jamal took in a sharp breath as her expert fingers tugged at the top button.

The light danced in her eyes. *This is a test. She wants to see how far I'll let her go.* After she opened the third button of his shirt, he raised his hands to stop her.

"Allie, I can't."

"Shh." Allie ignored his protests and brought her mouth to his, crushing him against her blood-red lips. She tasted like the root beer she'd been sipping.

"Allie, please," Jamal managed through their exchange of hot tongues and warm breath. "I have a wife at home."

"That's fine. I'm not looking for anything permanent. I want to warm you up, Jamal. All over." Jamal opened his mouth, and she covered it with hers. He didn't have the strength to fight. He wanted this. His arms wrapped around her, drawing her into him.

Jamal reached into her hair and pulled back her head, exposing her neck. He buried his face in the hollow of her throat, tasting the salt on her skin. He let go of her hair and used both hands, cupping the underside of her butt.

"Mmm, Jamal... Jamal..."

"Jamal? Oh."

His head shot up, horrified. "Hannah? Uh, wait a minute," he said, scrambling out of Allie's embrace. He pushed her away, twisting around her computer bag and snacks until he was on the far side of the room near his desk.

"I'll come back," the receptionist said. Her accusatory glare cut right through him.

"It's alright, Hannah. What is it?" Jamal wanted to ask her why she was looking at him the way she was and why she hadn't knocked when he'd drawn the blinds, but the words wouldn't come. He knew damn well why. She had busted him in the act. Hannah knew he was married—knew he had a step-daughter and a baby on the way too.

"Allie's client, Miss Lombardi, called. She said you two weren't answering your phones. She wants the house."

"That's great news," Allie said, clapping her hands together. She either didn't notice or didn't care that Hannah's lips had become a tight line.

"Thank you, Hannah." Jamal addressed her, making steady eye contact, as if things were business as usual. What else could he do? "Was there anything else?"

"That's it, Jamal. I assume you have her phone number?"

"Yes, I've got it," Allie said, scrolling through her contact list.

"Then I'll let you get back to it." Hannah shot him a reproving look, then closed the office door behind her.

"Shit. She knows my wife," Jamal said to Allie.

"Quiet, Jamal. Yes, Miss Lombardi, this is Allie Swanson.

How are you? My receptionist gave me the message that you called. Yes... that's right... nope, there's no need to fill out the consent form. The other buyers didn't think they could match your offer. That's right. You're the sole bidder." Allie gave Jamal a thumbs-up.

He sat at his desk with his head in his hands. Hannah knew Qaylah. What if she went to her desk and called her right now? Could his marriage be over before he arrived home for dinner? His finger throbbed as if it would burst. He needed more bandages, but there was no way in hell he'd ask now.

Why was he such an idiot? Was it worth throwing away his new wife and children for this slut? His stomach churned. He'd call it a night and go home to Qaylah, where he belonged.

"Jamal, you were right. Things are turning around. Miss Lombardi has agreed to buy the house. She's ecstatic now that there's no competition." Allie packed up her things and cleaned the crumbs off the tiny sofa.

"I have to go. She's coming to the office first thing in the morning. I should be fine. I know how to process everything, but I'll call you if I need something." She stopped at the door and turned back to him. "I don't think Hannah will say anything, Jamal. I suspect she's jealous that it wasn't her. Cheer up and go home to your wife. And try to keep warm." Allie blew him a kiss and left his office.

Jamal hopped into his car and sped onto the highway. It felt good to get out of the office and hit the road. The high speeds helped him breathe. Of all the stupid things he could have done, getting caught making out with a coworker by the receptionist had to be at the top. Qaylah would never forgive him. He felt like wringing Hannah's neck until it snapped. The nosy bitch thought she owned the place whenever Ashraf wasn't there. All she had to do was fucking knock. Was that so hard?

Jamal drove until he reached the condo that he and Tim were supposed to sell. It was the kind of place he wanted for his family. He and Tim hadn't had one meeting about it. The past few days were a nightmare. Everything was going to shit, and it all started with that fucking house. He drove away without going inside.

Various scenarios ran through his head. Had Hannah spilled the beans already? Would Qaylah forgive him? He'd have to convince her it was in the family's best interest to stay together.

Jamal loved her and wanted her to have a happy and safe pregnancy. She couldn't do that if her husband wasn't there to support her. Qaylah wasn't selfish like that. She'd stay.

He could smell Allie's perfume and taste her root beer kisses on his lips when he licked them. Even now, he wanted to taste more than her mouth. Despite the fear of losing his marriage, Allie roused an unquenched hunger inside him. He wasn't sure how he'd gotten involved with her in the first place, but it had to end. For Qaylah's sake. And the kids.

He clambered out of the Escalade and walked to the porch. There was a sense of foreboding as he climbed the stairs. The humid night air pressed his shirt into him, a sign that summer was around the corner.

If he saved his marriage, Jamal would take Qaylah and Katie across the state to Virginia Beach with the money he made from selling the house on Spiegel Road. They needed a vacation now more than ever.

Jamal opened the front door and stood between the two contrasting shades of darkness. The dim light of the streetlamp made the interior of the house look less inviting. Nervous fingers reached for the light switch. The rest of him refused to budge until he could see.

"As Salaamu Alaikum," Jamal said to the empty house.

Cold air hit him in the face as he stepped across the threshold. Fear pierced his heart. Was Qaylah right about last night? Had it been his overactive imagination? Had he scratched himself? His hand found the odd crescent shapes on his neck.

He punched his wife's phone number in his cellphone and waited. The sound of her voicemail sent him over the edge. Did Hannah tell?

"As Salaamu Alaikum. Qaylah, this is Jamal. Where are you? I'm home and you're not. It's kind of late for a pregnant woman and a three-year-old child to be out, don't you think? Anyway, call me back as soon as you get this message." He hung up and flopped down on the sofa with his computer bag.

Jamal leaned back and rested his head into the cushions. He couldn't remember the last time he sat on it, if at all. The sound of his breathing spooked him; the house was too quiet.

He adjusted his sitting position and retrieved his laptop. Since no one was here, he could squeeze in a few more hours of work. He'd sleep in before his appointment tomorrow. Qaylah would like that. If she didn't know about Allie.

Allie. He couldn't shake the nagging rise of his body temperature from their kiss. God bless whoever taught her how to kiss.

Jamal cocked his ear, listening to passing cars. A vehicle paused near the driveway, then kept going. It wasn't Qaylah.

He logged into his computer but couldn't concentrate on work. He searched for something more exciting in the private browser and slipped a hand into his unzipped pants. It wasn't something he did often, but tonight he couldn't release his built-up tension. After he spent himself, Jamal shut the laptop and tossed it onto the couch. The end of his bandage stuck to it and came off. *They don't make them like they used to.*

The cut on his finger had vanished with no hint of a scar.

He ran his fingers over his neck. Frowning, he double-checked. The moon-shaped scars had healed. But how?

Jamal rested his throbbing head on the overstuffed couch. What was going on? Gradually, he closed his eyes and sank deeper into the cushions. The hum of the air conditioner soothed him. For once, the room felt warm. His ears pricked up for a second. Was there someone laughing? Sleep took him.

CHAPTER FIFTEEN

"JAMAL. Jamal, wake up. Wake up right now." Qaylah hovered over Jamal and the bright overhead light burned rings into his retinas.

"As Salaamu Alaikum, Qaylah. I guess I fell asleep waiting for you."

"It looks like you were doing a heck of a lot more than waiting," Qaylah said, both hands on her hips. Jamal thought about how many times his mother had taken that stance when he was in trouble. He rubbed his eyes, coaxing them to focus. His wife stood over him, fiery red curls blazing.

"What did you do to your hair?"

"Never mind. What is that on your computer?"

Jamal turned towards her pointing finger, and his heart leapt into his throat. "Why are you going through my things? I closed this," he said, shutting the screen as fast as he could manage.

"Nothing? You call porn nothing, Jamal? What's wrong with you? Are you bored with our marriage?"

"No. Answer my question. Why were you snooping on my computer?"

"It was wide open on the coffee table, playing that filth

when we got here. How could you do this in our home? What if Katie saw?"

Thank God. "She didn't, though."

"How do you know?" She tossed her new hairdo from one side of her head to the other. The light made her look rusty. Red didn't suit her one bit.

"I know she didn't see it because you would have mentioned it if she had. Look," he said, rising off the sofa. "I was waiting for you to get home and I was in the mood. But, like I said, I put the computer away. I didn't even finish watching a video." He looked her in the eyes. Technically, it was true. He hadn't needed to finish watching it.

"Why are your pants undone?"

"Qaylah...."

She turned to walk away. He caught up with her near the bottom of the stairs. "Qaylah don't leave. Honestly, I did nothing wrong. I was going to, but I changed my mind." His father once told him that it wasn't a bad deed to lie if it kept the peace.

"Are you telling me the truth, Jamal?" Qaylah's brow furrowed, and Jamal did his best not to wince at her ugly hair. He hoped it was a semi-permanent dye.

"Of course, baby. Come here, let me see your beautiful hair." Now that he'd gotten away with the first one, the lies slipped out of his mouth with ease. He could handle her being upset about the sex video for a few days if she didn't know about Allie.

They both jumped when someone knocked on the door.

"It's eleven-thirty," Qaylah said, frowning.

Jamal fastened his pants and belt and walked to the door. "Who is it?"

"Is Kylah Cavanaugh here?" A male voice asking for his

wife at this time of night. Jamal turned to Qaylah to ask what was up and saw the dread on her face.

Jamal unlocked the door and snatched it open. "Hey, man, what do you want with my wife?"

"Tell her it's her ex-husband, Brian. I need to see her right away."

JAMAL LOOKED the man at the door up and down. His scraggly hair hung to his shoulders, and he wore a pair of black jeans and a t-shirt. A plaid shirt sat tied at his waist. Brian. He looked like a regular guy you'd pass on the street, never thinking twice about him.

Qaylah made her ex-husband sound like he was one step away from starvation. This guy looked like he bench-pressed two-fifty without a problem. Jamal checked out the car at the end of the drive. It didn't look like something a drug addict would own. Jamal's sister owned the same make and model.

"What are you doing here?" Jamal rubbed his thumb over the healed spot of his finger. He was glad to have full use of his hands in case things got out of control.

"I need to talk to Kylah," Brian said.

"It's pronounced Qaylah now," he said, stressing the Arabic accent. "What do you want to talk about?"

"I want to apologize and check on my little girl."

"Sorry, man. It's late—"

"It's alright, Jamal. I'm here." Qaylah ducked under Jamal's arm and stood between the men. "Brian. You look... clean and sober. Who told you where I lived?" She finished fastening her hijab pin and folded her arms.

Jamal studied his wife's body language. He expected

Qaylah to feel scared or annoyed. Not curious. Either way, he was here to protect her.

"I got out of rehab six months ago and found work. Listen, do you folks mind if we talk inside? I don't plan to stay long, but it's a little awkward talking this way."

"We can hear you fine," Jamal said.

"He's right, Jamal. Let's hear what he has to say. You have five minutes, Brian."

~

"THANKS, KYLAH."

"It's Qaylah," Jamal said, correcting Brian's pronunciation. They sat at the kitchen table, jabbing at dry slices of grocery store cake.

"Since when?" Brian asked.

"Since I converted. It seemed like the logical choice to switch from Kylah to Qaylah, right?"

"I guess," Brian said. "I can't pronounce it, so please forgive me for reverting to the former version."

"She invited you into our home. The least you could do is try to say her name correctly," Jamal said.

"Whoa. Jamal, right? I'm not some asshole—"

"Language."

"Sorry, Ky, didn't mean to offend. I'm not some jerk who gets off on micro-aggressions. I legit can't pronounce the letter, even after learning Arabic in Iraq, and Lord knows I tried."

"You were in Iraq?" Jamal leaned back in the hard kitchen chair. "Killing innocent people for the U.S. Government."

"I did my best to avoid it, brother. Why do you think I ended up on drugs in the first place?"

Qaylah held up a finger. "Guys, we can discuss politics

some other time. Tell me why you're here, Brian, and why did you come so late?"

"I worked a double shift today at the printing press and I have to be back there bright and early. Your mother reached out and told me where to find you, Ky."

"Why, to rescue me from the big bad Muslim? Did she say that I need to turn me back into a good Christian girl and see the error of my ways?"

"A little of both, but that's not why I'm here. I came here to apologize."

Qaylah stared at Brian like he had two heads. She pushed away her plate of cake and burst into tears.

"Qaylah, I can send him away if you need me to," Jamal said. *Who did this guy think he was, barging in on his family? He could take his apology and shove it.*

"You've never done that before," Qaylah said, reaching for a napkin.

"No, I've never apologized. I've never admitted my mistakes or how much I hurt you and that beautiful little girl." Brian sighed and ran his hands through his thick blonde hair. "I couldn't let go of my addiction, Q-Kylah. See, man, I can't say it."

Jamal shrugged.

"I let you down, Ky. I know that. It was a good thing that I went to rehab. A blessing. Had I not checked myself in when my daddy passed—"

"Your daddy is dead?" Qaylah's hands flew to her mouth. "I'm so sorry, Brian."

"It's okay, Ky. Daddy was tired." The three adults turned to the kitchen entrance, where Katie stood with Mister Sniffles. "Who is he, Mama?"

Brian's chair legs scraped against the floor as he stood and scooped up Katie. Jamal stood too. Qaylah grabbed his arm.

"I'm your daddy. How's my baby girl doing?" Brian showered Katie's face and hair with kisses. "You're so big, Jellybean. Did your Mama tell you I named you that? Daddy loves you more than you will ever know. You're the only reason I'm a better man today."

Jamal and Qaylah looked on as Brian sniffed Katie's hair and stroked it with his hands. "Thank you, Jesus," he said, rocking the girl back and forth. His eyes flew open and spotted Jamal. "Oh, shit—"

"Language," Qaylah said.

"Shoot, man, I'm sorry. I meant thank you, Lord. I didn't mean any disrespect in your house."

"How long are you staying?" Jamal asked.

"Don't be rude, Jamal," Qaylah said.

"I'm about to hit the road. Ky, I need to finish my apology."

"Go ahead," she said. "Do you want some coffee or tea?"

"No thanks. I'll never get to sleep if I have caffeine. Darling, why don't you sit in the chair with your mama?" Brian directed Katie, who turned and strode over to Qaylah.

"Mama's having a baby," she said from the comfort of her mother's lap.

Qaylah stiffened and glanced at Jamal.

"That's wonderful, sweetie. You'll have two brothers or sisters, or maybe one of each." Brian turned to Qaylah and Jamal. "Congratulations."

"It's too soon to speculate about twins," Qaylah said.

Brian laughed. "Natalia, my fiancée, is pregnant, too. I wasn't going to say anything because it happened so fast, but you know how hard it is for me to keep a secret."

"You're having a baby, too?" Katie's eyes grew wide.

"That's right, Jellybean."

"When did this happen? When is she due?" Qaylah asked.

"She's three months pregnant. We've been together officially for two."

"Oh...." Qaylah's voice trailed off like it did whenever she was about to cry. Jamal wondered why the news would upset her.

"Congratulations," Jamal said, smiling. He felt a lot better knowing someone else needed this dirtbag.

"Thanks, Jamal. What was I saying? Oh, yeah. Daddy passed on and we read the will. He left me a windfall—can you believe it? The old man was sitting on a treasure. I put it in the bank before I checked myself into rehab. When I got out, I settled my affairs and reopened The Inkpot."

"Ink spot?" Katie asked.

"Inkpot. It's a book printing service that your grandfather owned," Brian told her. "I'll take you for a tour if you want."

"Okay," Katie said, snuggling into her mother.

"How'd you have time to meet someone and run a business?" Qaylah asked.

"Natalia and I met on site. She gave me a tour of the machinery and the rest is history. She's the general manager at the press and my right hand. I couldn't run it without her."

"I see. It's getting late, Brian." Qaylah scooted her chair backwards and put Katie down.

"It is. I apologize for coming over here like this, but I couldn't hold on to what wasn't mine any longer. Here you go." Brian stood and dug a fat envelope out of his back pocket and gave it to Qaylah.

"What's this?" She opened the envelope and slammed it shut. "This isn't drug money, is it?"

"No, Ky, it isn't. I told you, I inherited a large sum from my daddy's passing. That money is the back child support I owe and a little extra from my own pocket. I put some aside for Katie in a bank account for when she grows up. I want her to go to the school of her choice and not worry about money like we did. I'll send you the particulars of the bank account tomorrow."

Qaylah wiped a tear from her cheek. "Brian, I don't know what to say," she placed her hand on her heart.

"You don't have to say anything. I hope this isn't out of line, but I want to say, I love your red hair, Ky. It's awesome."

"How about both of you say goodnight?" Jamal jerked his head towards the door.

CHAPTER SIXTEEN

THE NEXT MORNING, Jamal got up with the sun. The tapping sound in the bathroom walls woke him. When he couldn't ignore it any longer, he threw back the duvet and went to investigate. Rats in the walls would be par for the course in this place.

An icy gust of air met him as he opened the door. It was colder than the rest of the house here. *Ghosts.* He cracked a smile and thought of Allie.

The tapping grew louder, echoing in his ears, tinny and hollow, like he was standing in a metal tube as someone banged on the outside with a stick. His head hurt. The rhythm of the tapping matched the throbbing in his finger.

Jamal watched beads of blood form where the scar used to be. He brought his hand closer to his face, peering at it under the light. Something wriggled under the surface.

"Good morning." Qaylah waltzed into the bathroom and lifted the toilet lid. "How about you give me just a minute?" she asked.

"I was here first," Jamal said.

"You either let me use the toilet or clean up the mess," she said.

"Have it your way, princess," he said, storming out of the bathroom. *Such entitlement.* He felt betrayed from last night.

Qaylah had invited Brian to visit Katie whenever he wanted. Jamal thought it was a crazy suggestion. How could she trust that he was telling the truth? She didn't even discuss it with him first.

"She's his daughter, Jamal. I don't see why it concerns you," she said when they lay in bed.

"She's my stepdaughter, Qaylah, of course I have a say. He can't guarantee that his life will stay on track, and I don't want him around the house until he can. For now, he needs supervised visits when I'm around so that I can keep him in check."

"You're being silly, Jamal."

"Am I?"

"Yes. Brian has gone through rehab and he's settling down with his girlfriend. He's never cared about Katie before. This is a good sign."

"Are you sure you aren't trying to keep him coming around for yourself?"

"For me?" Qaylah scoffed. "You're sounding jealous."

Jamal opened his eyes and glanced at the silhouette of his wife in the dark bedroom. "Why would I be jealous?"

"That's what I want to know. Brian is acting like a normal person, but I know he's unreliable. In time, his true nature will resurface, but for Katie's sake, I'll keep the peace." She reached out for him and squeezed his hand. "Before I forget, I have a doctor's appointment in the afternoon. I need you to pick up Katie from preschool."

"Why do you wait until the last minute to tell me these things? I'm busier than ever, Qaylah. I don't know if I can step away from work at your whim."

"I texted you a reminder weeks ago when I made the appointment, Jamal."

"Don't change the subject," he said. "Why were you upset that he had a girlfriend?"

Her body stiffened. "I wasn't."

"Don't lie, Qaylah. You're not good at it. I saw the way you looked when he said his girlfriend was pregnant. Why did it upset you? Did you forget you were married?"

"Sure, I was upset, but it's perfectly natural. It seems to me you're the one who forgot. Remember that filth you were watching—with your pants open?"

"Let's not start that again. At least the people in the video aren't real."

"Of course, they're real. They're living people doing disgusting things for other people's pleasure."

"I can't believe you were married to that guy," Jamal said, ignoring her. "He was a soldier in Iraq. Do you know what they did to innocent people over there?"

"Yes, Jamal. I know. Did you forget that I'm part of the charity committee? We send supplies to refugees every month. I don't need your lectures on the horrors the Iraqi people face."

"You would have let him into the house if I weren't here, wouldn't you? I'll bet that money made you sweet on him again, didn't it? Let me guess, he had you at hello?"

"What's gotten into you?"

"Nothing. Go to sleep, Qaylah." She huffed and turned away from him.

Jamal stared into the darkness, waiting for his mind to stop thinking about the other redheaded woman in his life. The real one. Qaylah was a good wife who tried her best to be an upstanding member of the community. His family loved her, hell, she spent more time with them than he did. He loved her.

If all of that was true, why was he thinking about Allie? Why was he wondering how good she was in bed? Why did he want more than a kiss?

No matter how he tried, Jamal couldn't shake his thoughts of her. She intoxicated him. His body tingled as he remembered how she pulled him to her lips and caressed his face.

THE SCENT of French toast wafted upstairs through the air ducts, competing for the attention of his senses. For now, he fought hard not to think of Allie and stay in the present. *I love my wife.*

Jamal bent over the sink and spat peppermint-flavored mouthwash into it. He wiped his beard dry then checked his teeth. For real estate agents, image mattered. Ashraf was right.

He reached into his pocket and pulled out the card Chauncey gave him. It couldn't hurt. Just a trim to make his face look more streamlined.

"Jamal, breakfast."

"Coming," he said, cutting out the bathroom light before he trotted down the stairs. He heard tapping in the walls but didn't have time to check.

"Breakfast is ready. I made French toast."

"It smells good," he said, taking his seat. "Hey, Jellybean. How's it going?"

Katie eyed him with suspicion. The girl hadn't spoken to him in days. Jamal resented it. How could she be ignoring him but not her junkie father?

"The weather's warming up, isn't it?" Qaylah said, looking out the window into the backyard. "We should spend more time outside."

"I agree," Jamal said. "I was thinking about taking some time off work. We could take a trip to Virginia Beach with Katie, maybe rent a condo, and make the most of it." He cut a piece of his toast and slathered it with butter and syrup.

"I don't think that's a good idea, Jamal."

He sighed and laid down his fork. "Why not? It's a great idea. We can go as soon as I sell this house and the condo. I need to meet with my team and get it done, but it shouldn't be a problem. It might take another week or so, and you'd be in between doctor's appointments."

"I don't want to go to the beach and expose Katie to all of those people wearing inappropriate clothing."

"Are you serious? What those people wear is none of our business Qaylah, and I expect them to feel the same way about us. Katie will learn eventually to not pay those people any attention."

"No. I would feel uncomfortable at the beach."

"We could rent a house then. One with access to a private beach. And a pool," he said.

"How can we afford it? We're saving up to buy a house, remember? We can't stay in this place much longer. It's falling apart."

Jamal drank the last of his orange juice, then wiped the corners of his mouth with a napkin. Why was she being bitchy? He chalked it up to hormones. "What about the money that Brian gave you?"

"What about it?"

"How much was it?"

"Why?"

"It looked like a nice stack of cash. How much was it?"

"A lot," she said.

"You should count it."

Qaylah rubbed an invisible spot on the counter with the dishrag. "What for?"

"Don't you want to know how much he gave you? And you need to know how much it is before you deposit it into the bank," Jamal said. He picked up the newspaper and turned to the real estate listings but didn't read them. Instead, he watched Qaylah's back, reading her body language.

"I'll count it later. I'm in no hurry."

"Of course. But I was thinking we could use some of it to help... with the vacation... if you want to," Jamal said.

Qaylah threw the dish towel into the sink. "Can't you afford the vacation? It was your idea."

"It's something for us to consider, Qaylah."

"No, it's something you've already considered. It's my money, Jamal. I'm not obligated to share it with you."

Jamal scratched an itch in his beard. "You don't have to be like that, Qaylah. I can pay for the vacation. I pay for everything around here, anyway."

"Good. That's what you're supposed to do."

Jamal crumpled the paper, adding new creases in the middle of the page, making it difficult to fold. He gave up trying and slammed it on the table. Katie jumped and slid the cereal box in front of her face, blocking her view of him.

"Go get the envelope."

"No."

"I said get it."

"I won't."

"Is this what you call obedience?"

Qaylah turned and pointed her finger at him. "I will not give it to you. It's none of your business how much money is in that envelope."

Jamal sprang to his feet, knocking over the chair and the carton of orange juice. Juice landed at Qaylah's feet, splashing her dress. His words came out in a deafening boom. "Go get it!" Katie clapped her hands over her ears. He ignored her sobbing.

"Eighty-six thousand, five-hundred dollars," Qaylah said. "The idiot brought me an envelope with more cash than I've ever seen in my life." She sat down at the table and pulled Katie into her lap. "Brian owed me two-thousand dollars in back child support."

Jamal picked up the chair and sat down hard. "Eighty-grand, huh? That must have been some windfall."

Qaylah didn't respond.

"He must still be in love with you. No guy would give a woman he doesn't want that kind of money. Even if they share a kid."

She narrowed her eyes.

"No offense, Qaylah. I love you, but I'd never let you loose with eighty-grand. We can sit down when I get home and make a financial plan for you."

"I have dominion over my money, you have dominion over yours," she said. "I'll talk to my financial adviser at the bank, thank you. Also, I would appreciate it if you wouldn't play with your beard at the table, you're getting hairs everywhere. It's disgusting."

Jamal opened his mouth to reply, then closed it and removed his hand from his chin. "Fine." He stood and wiped the stray hairs onto the floor. "Have it your way, Qaylah. If you think you can handle your finances on your own, be my guest. It's one less worry for me." He shoved the chair under the table, knocking the cereal box backwards, splaying multi-grain circles into the stream of spilled juice.

"Great," Qaylah said, folding her arms and shooting him a dirty look.

Jamal put on his watch, ignoring her. "Have a good day, Jellybean. I'll see you later." He bent down to kiss the little girl on top of her head and pretended not to notice her flinch.

CHAPTER SEVENTEEN

JAMAL FLOORED IT, racing the Escalade down the highway. He had to get to the house before his first showing and traffic was heavy. "Let's go," he said, honking his horn.

Qaylah had some nerve. How could she think so poorly of him? Her using some of the money to pay for their vacation was simply a suggestion. He would have paid her back. Jamal was a self-made man, successful at his job. Taking care of his family was a source of pride. She had looked at him like he was a thief or a playboy looking for a sugar mama.

He blamed Brian for this. Why did he have to show up unannounced on his doorstep in the middle of the night? Couldn't he come at a decent hour? The devil loved to disrupt a happy home.

Qaylah left Brian for Katie's sake. That was no secret. She leaned in whatever direction suited the child. If Brian pretended that he wanted Katie, how soon would Qaylah run back to him?

Katie looked at Jamal like he was the devil incarnate, but why? Again, he blamed Brian. Just when they were stable and happy, he comes back into the picture to disrupt and confuse them. Brian could try it, but he would fail. They were his girls now.

Fifteen minutes later, he was parked outside the house on Spiegel feeling pleased. With all the strange happenings in the past few days, the crew had gone above and beyond the call of duty to provide damage control.

A knock at the door surprised him. His showing with Asad and Sarah was in thirty minutes. He shrugged. They lived closer to Spiegel and could get here without slogging through traffic like he did. Jamal opened the door and his shoulders sagged.

"What do you want, Tobias? I have people coming to look at the house."

"Sorry to bother you. I can't find Buck."

"What else is new? I think he spends more time away from you than with you." Jamal didn't blame the dog for that. "If I see your dog, I'll let you know, okay? Now get out of here before the buyers see you and change their minds."

"I hope you ain't selling the house to weirdos. That includes women. If they come in pairs, especially Black women, turn them away."

"Goodbye, Tobias." Jamal closed the door in his face and went back to sit and wait at the small workspace in the living room. He took out his computer and booted it up. The adult website stared him in the face.

"Shit." He closed the website and pulled up the home page displaying his business logo in its place. A knock sounded at the door. "In the nick of time," he said.

Jamal swung open the door and smiled at the short couple. "As Salaamu Alaikum, Asad and Sarah. Welcome."

"Wa Alaikum As Salaam," they responded. Jamal ushered them inside the house and closed the door behind them.

"How was the traffic?" he asked.

"It wasn't bad," Sarah replied. "Asad was grading papers

the whole time, so it wouldn't have mattered to him if it were fast or slow," she said.

"You're still driving?" Jamal asked, noting her pregnant condition.

"I am. The doctor says as long as I can fit behind the steering wheel, I can zoom around town," she said, rubbing her belly.

"Don't let her fool you, Jamal. I'm the one making the midnight runs to get chili cheese fries and milkshakes."

"From Syreeta's?"

"That's right."

"Ha. Don't let Asad fool you, Jamal. Most of those midnight visits are his idea. He gets empathy cravings," Sarah said, rubbing Asad's matching belly.

"Guilty as charged," Asad said. "But how can I resist? They have the best double cheeseburgers and chocolate milkshakes."

"Wow, I think I need a milkshake now," Jamal said.

"Me too," Asad said.

Visiting Syreeta's for milkshakes and ice cream was a favorite Saturday evening pastime for his family. He'd neglected doing it for a few weeks. Life was too damned busy.

"Would you like to start at the top and work our way down?" Jamal asked Sarah. "The steps aren't steep, but I leave it up to you."

"Let's start at the top and work our way down," she agreed.

"After you," Jamal said. Things were looking up. Asad and Sarah were just the right couple to buy this house. They had stable income and were looking to get out from under their in-laws and parents. This house was the perfect solution. Jamal saw dollar signs as he trotted upstairs.

∾

"I LOVE IT, Jamal. This house has everything we need," Sarah said. Her large, dark eyes crinkled at the corners when she smiled. Jamal hoped Qaylah would glow like that as her pregnancy progressed.

"Slow down, Sarah. She's buying the place, and we haven't checked out the basement yet."

"Or the beautiful front yard. Did you see that gorgeous willow tree? I can picture our children playing there one day," Sarah said.

An image of Sarah feeling the heartbeat of the tree the way Allie had described flashed in Jamal's mind. He frowned. This couple wouldn't be doing that superstitious shit. He opened the basement door and flipped the light switch. "Watch your step," he said, pointing to the small staircase.

Sarah went first. "Check it out, Asad. The basement is perfect. And it's clean down here too."

"Do the washer and dryer come with the house?" Asad asked.

"They do. The kitchen appliances are new and there's a riding mower that the owner threw in as well."

"Sweet," Asad said, scratching the thin patch of hair at the top of his head. "Is there a shed?"

"Yup. It's a big one. You'll love it."

"That's exciting. I'd like to build a workshop—"

"Asad! Asad!" Sarah clamped her mouth with her hand.

"Sarah?" Asad pulled his wife away from the laundry facilities. "Ya Allah. Jamal, what's that stench?"

"Let me see," Jamal said. He crouched to inspect the dryer. He pushed the door open with the tip of a pencil. A blackish-red liquid seeped out from the liner, and dripped down the dryer's window in thick, congealed clumps, landing on a dog collar on the floor. Buck's collar.

"Is-is that a... dog?" Asad stepped closer to Jamal with his shirt pulled over his nose.

"I think so," Jamal said, clutching his stomach. "I have to call the police," he said, pushing the door closed with the pencil tip. "Guys, I'm sorry about this. Let's get you out of here. Sarah, you can use the sink in the kitchen to clean up."

The couple retreated from the basement in haste. Jamal stared at the dryer in disbelief. Who the fuck would do something like this? What kind of twisted individual was he dealing with?

Jamal stood and nudged the dryer closed with the tip of his shoe until he heard it click, then opened all the basement windows to air out the room. At least the seal of the dryer door kept the smell contained.

A glint of light in the corner caught his eye. Jamal approached the object and bent down to retrieve it from under the hot water heater.

"What the hell?" Jamal turned the object over in his hands. It was the figurine—the same one that cut him, except it was intact. *Maybe it's another one.* The cracks in the body, sealed with glue, disagreed with his assessment. Someone had fixed the old one and left it there.

Jamal sighed and dropped it into his pocket while he searched through the dozen business cards in his card holder until he found Officer Parker's number. Tobias was going to cause a shitstorm over his dead dog. The poor bastard.

From a basement window, he heard two car doors slam and a vehicle pull out of the driveway. Jamal shook his head. He'd let the police deal with Tobias. In the meantime, he had to find a buyer, dead dog, or no dead dog.

"LORD, Almighty. What kind of sick bastard would put a dog in the dryer?" Officer Parker took off his sunglasses and used his nightstick to close the dryer door. "Have you ever smelled a dead body, Mister Jackson?"

"No, I haven't," Jamal said, blinking back tears. Officer Parker had given him some menthol rub to put under his nose, but it burned more than it masked the smell.

"The stink is something else, isn't it? It's shocking because it hits you all at once when you open the dryer door." Officer Parker ushered Jamal up the stairs and closed the basement door. "The entire house is gonna need to air out now. I'd hold off showing it for at least a week, so folks don't see the flies if I were you. I'll send a forensics team over to investigate. They'll probably want to take the dryer back to the lab."

"That's fine with me," Jamal said. The sooner he got the mess out of the house, the better. He'd have to owe Ashraf for the appliance. He wondered when his boss was coming back from Pakistan with his mother.

Maybe he could buy a used dryer in the same make and model and have it installed. Ashraf could hear about the entire ordeal later; he wouldn't care what happened in the house if it sold for a good price.

Jamal and Officer Parker stepped out of the house and drew fresh air into their lungs. "You keep a lockbox on the door, right?"

"Yes. It's right here," Jamal said, pointing to the large metal and plastic box.

"Who has access to this place? You and who else?"

"Landscapers, cleaners, repairmen. They've been in and out for about two weeks, getting the house ready for showing."

"I'm gonna need a list of everyone who came in or out in the past twenty-four hours."

"I can do that," Jamal said. "I can't believe this is happening."

"First the birds, now this."

Jamal nodded. "I've had a lot of trouble with this property, man. This was the first client who actually saw it. I thought for sure I'd be filling out paperwork and handing them the keys in a few weeks. They loved it until we got to the fucking basement."

"It looks like your troubles aren't over," Officer Parker said.

Jamal followed the cop's eyes. The door to the house next door swung open. Tobias was coming. Shit.

"Let me handle this, Mister Jackson. He's gonna lose it."

Officer Parker jogged to meet Tobias on his own property. Jamal retreated into the house and closed the screen door. He listened to the wind chimes hanging on the porch, swaying in the gentle breeze while he waited. It didn't take long for the old man to lose it.

"No! What did that nigger do to my dog? I'm gonna kill him! Buck... Buck!" Jamal listened to the grieving howls coming from Tobias. He couldn't help but liken Tobias's sobs to a heartbroken old dog.

"It's a minor setback," Jamal said.

"Setback for what?"

Jamal jumped when he heard the woman's voice. The first thing he saw when he stared out the open window was the shock of red hair and freckled skin. He hadn't noticed her standing on the lawn. "Allie?"

"Who?"

Jamal focused his eyes on the tall light-skinned Black woman with long red locs and frowned. He was seeing Allie everywhere. "Sorry, I mistook you for someone else."

The woman smiled. "She must be good looking," she said, climbing the porch steps.

Jamal's lips spread, and he opened his mouth in a full grin. "Almost as good as you," he said through the window.

"Nice recovery. I'm Officer Tasha Macklin."

"Sure. Give me one sec." He jogged to the door and opened it for her. She showed him her badge and he stepped back to let her inside.

"I heard you have a special treat inside a dryer for me."

"Afraid so. Officer Parker said you'd be willing to take the dryer away."

"Let me have a look first. Poor Buck," she said.

"You're familiar with Buck?"

"I'm familiar with the cats Buck liked to tear apart under the willow tree," she said, stepping into the house.

"It sounds like Buck may have created some enemies."

"You don't know the half of it," Officer Macklin said, putting down a cumbersome-looking black case. "Tobias and Buck had run-ins with all the previous homeowners of this house."

"All? I wasn't aware the property had multiple owners."

"It wasn't official. The Frauenhaus clan passed this house down from woman to woman until they tired of it or died in it. If that happened, they held a ritual under the willow trees to determine the next woman in line. My mama said their deity didn't like male energy."

"Frauenhaus?"

"They called this place Frauenhaus, 'Women's House.' The name is German, but the inhabitants were Black descendants of slaves. They were in dispute with Tobias's family for many years. Tobias claims they stole the land from his ancestor," Officer Macklin said. "Forgive me if I forget the details."

"It figures Tobias had something to do with it," Jamal said.

"Tobias wasn't always this way. I've heard that he was a

somewhat reasonable person before Vietnam. Dealing with Tobias has been interesting."

"I can imagine," Jamal said.

"Things got out of hand towards the latter years, right before the family broke up. I have nothing against cats, but I wished they'd gotten her fixed so Buck would stay—" A loud bang interrupted them.

"Was that a blown tire?" Jamal asked.

Officer Macklin took off out the front door. Jamal followed, but she waved him back.

"Get back inside, Sir. That was a gunshot." He nodded when he saw her drawn handgun. She checked multiple directions for a shooter, then skittered down the porch towards his vehicle. Jamal paused in the doorway when he saw Officer Parker emerge from the house next door, his arms covered in blood.

"Call the coroner," he said, doubling over. Jamal watched him clutch his kneecaps and gag.

"Do we need an ambulance?" she asked, holstering her weapon.

"There's no hurry," Officer Parker said. "The damn fool killed himself."

CHAPTER EIGHTEEN

"GODDAMN, Jamal. You're having the shittiest month. I can't believe that the codger shot himself in the head." Tim swiveled in his chair in the conference room. He pulled Jamal aside as soon as he got to the office and demanded they have a sit-down to discuss strategies for selling the condo.

Tim was the last person he wanted to talk to after a day like today. Jamal confided in him about the suicide, hoping Tim would feel some empathy and leave him alone. Instead, he'd hailed Renee, Chauncey, and Allie for an informal meeting.

Jamal noted the time. This was the usual time slot for team meetings, so why not?

"Nobody's gonna want that house when the news blabs about the dead guy next door," Chauncey said.

"Hey, Jamal, you can sell that one too," Renee said, laughing at her own joke.

"That's cold, Renee. You know he's stressed. You should give it to me, Jamal. I've got a cousin who will buy anything. He'll pay more if he knows a guy offed himself next door," Tim said, scrolling through his phone. "Hell, he might buy both."

"Man, nobody's gonna want it. A dead dog in the dryer?" Chauncey held up his hands in disbelief.

"Dead dog? What dead dog? You mentioned the suicide

but didn't say shit about a dog." Tim turned to Jamal for an answer, and Renee put her phone down, giving Jamal her full attention.

"Hannah said the police called to get the lockbox records. Jamal showed the house and found a burnt dog in the dryer," Chauncey said.

"That's some horror movie shit," Tim said. "Forget what I said. My cousin won't buy it now. A dead dog is a bad omen."

"You are superstitious to the bone. I like that," Renee said, hitting Tim in the shoulder with her pack of tarot cards. "But you're right. Only a twisted person would want that house, unless it's someone who knows how to get rid of bad juju," she said.

"Who would kill a dog—like that?" Tim asked.

"Sorry, player," Chauncey said, rising from his seat. "You ain't ever selling that house. Ashraf will have to call on a higher power to take it off his hands when he gets back."

"He won't be happy," Renee said, getting up. "It sounds to me like you've been cursed. That house is a crossroad for spirits. I felt them when I was there. You should find out who you offended and ask for forgiveness. And learn how to treat people." She followed Chauncey out of the room.

Jamal released some of the tension in his jaw when they left.

"She's pretty open to weird stuff." Allie spoke up for the first time since they'd taken their seats at the table.

"I like weird stuff. Too bad she's not into men," Tim said.

"It figures," Jamal said, gritting his teeth.

"Don't worry, Jamal. You'll find someone to buy it. I have faith in you." Allie's smile traveled from her lips to her eyes, and he got lost in them for a moment.

"Bullshit," Tim said, using a rolled-up piece of paper to

amplify his voice. "Count your losses, Jamal. Nobody wants to live in a dog murder house next to a suicide house."

Jamal drank from his coffee cup and grimaced as he forced the cold liquid down his throat. "Tim's right, Allie. It's going to be near impossible to sell it."

"Damn right," Tim said.

"Near impossible—not impossible," Jamal said.

"You can do it, Jamal. I have faith in you."

"Why? He hasn't sold a thing in the last three weeks. In this business, you're as good as your last sale." Tim sat back in his chair and grinned. "You should hold the door for him on your way out."

Jamal flashed Tim a dangerous look. "That's enough, Tim."

"She needs to hear the truth from somebody. You're hyping her up and she's doing the same shit to you. You're setting each other up for a hard fall."

"Ignore him, Allie. Tim, you said you wanted to meet me and Allie to talk about selling the condo. Do you want to get started or keep wasting time?"

Tim shrugged. "Let's get started."

THEY BRAINSTORMED FOR FORTY MINUTES, then convened at the condo. Tim separated himself from the group, darting around, taking pictures of the exterior. Jamal tried to tag along, but Tim evaded him at every turn.

"Tim is going crazy," she said, watching his tall frame bend over the pool to inspect the tiles. "Look at him go."

"Yeah, he's competitive. He wants the other corner office."

"He's threatened by you and Chauncey."

"Tim's a good salesman but out of his league this time."

"From what I've heard, he sells houses to his relatives. His resources are probably all tapped out."

"Relatives have friends," Jamal said.

"Mine don't. They prefer to stick with their own."

"Your family is close-knit?"

"You could say that. We come from the mystical mountains of North Carolina. I moved here when I was a teenager, so I don't consider myself a Virginian."

"No? Even after all this time?"

She lifted her hand to use it as a visor from the harsh sun. "All the happy times I remember happened in North Carolina. My family never had much success here. We grew up poor and isolated."

"I'm sorry to hear that."

"What about you?"

"Me? My family is close but I'm sort of the black sheep. I grew up in the suburbs with my mom and dad and siblings. I'm not from Virginia either."

"Oh yeah? Where are you from?"

"Rhode Island."

"You're far from home."

"That's right. If there's a tree beating for me, it's up north." Allie smiled at the reference.

"You never know," she said. "The tree's heart beats in the place you'll live for the rest of your life. No matter how many times you leave, it will always be there waiting."

"Unless they cut it down," Jamal said.

"You're going to argue no matter what I say, aren't you?" Her words sounded confrontational, but her smile said otherwise. Jamal watched her mouth as the corners of it flattened. "I think about you all the time. I'm not sure what to make of it."

His smile faded. "I think you should move on to someone else. I'm a married man, Allie. It would cause a lot of damage if we continued doing whatever this is." The words came out thick and difficult. He didn't want to say them at all, but what could he do?

"That wasn't what I wanted to hear," she said.

"I know. It wasn't what I wanted to say. If we'd met a year ago, I wouldn't put an end to it, but I'd marry you first."

"Marry me? I don't want to get married," she said. "I don't need a piece of paper to represent my feelings."

"Neither do I, but marriage is for protecting women."

"Who says I need protection? I can take care of myself."

"It gives you financial security and companionship. Doesn't every woman want to be a man's special lady?"

"Once I have my house back, I'll be my own special lady."

"What did you say?"

"Remember? I want to buy my parents' old house."

"I thought you gave up on that dream?"

"Changed my mind. I was a fool to think it didn't matter anymore, Jamal. I love my family and have decided that I'll do whatever it takes to get it back."

Jamal shuddered. Something about the way she explained it made him uneasy. "How come you want it so bad? You could make memories in a new place."

"My parents sold the house to pay off their debts, but they didn't get enough money for it. We had to move into a real dump after that, and they were murdered right before my sixteenth birthday."

His jaw dropped. "I'm sorry to hear that, Allie. Truly."

"Thanks, Jamal. I've been on my own for a long time, but the memories still sting. They wouldn't allow me to live with my older brothers and I ended up in foster care for a few years."

"How come?"

"We weren't mature enough to live on our own at the

time." Allie wiped a tear that escaped from the corner of her eye. "Look at me, crying at work."

"Don't worry about that. You've had your share of tragedy. I can't blame you for being attached to the house," Jamal said.

"I need to come up with buyers for these two houses, and soon. I can't delay. Tell me what to do and I will help you and Tim get this place ready to sell, too. It'll look good if I contribute something noteworthy, especially if I can win Tim's approval."

"We're in this together, Allie. We're gonna make it happen."

"You're in a constant state of optimism. Thanks, Jamal." She reached up and brushed his cheek with a quick motion from her fingertips. Her face darkened, and she withdrew her hand. "You don't think the police will blame me for what happened to that dog, do you?"

Jamal furrowed his brow. "Why would they do that?"

"I threatened to call animal control because it bit me," she said. "I might be a suspect."

"I wouldn't worry about it. Tobias had a lot of enemies. Any of them could have done that."

"Hey, losers. I need you to remove the lockbox. I forgot the code," Tim said, waving to them from the front door.

He reached inside his pants pocket to remove whatever was weighing it down.

"What's that? It's covered in dust and pocket lint." Allie inspected the clay figurine between her fingers, then blew on it. "I have a friend who is Shi'a. She prays on these clay stones. Is this the same thing? Do you pray with this?" She clutched it to her breast and closed her eyes.

Jamal furrowed his brow. "Are you whispering something? What are you doing?"

"I'm saying a prayer on it."

"Stop that," he said, wrangling it out of her hands. "You don't pray with this. It's something I found at the house on Spiegel."

"Oh, then I guess you should toss it."

"Yeah, I'll do it later," he said, putting it back in his pants pocket. The clay felt warm, as if it had been sitting in the sun all day. It was silly, but he felt better with it close to him. He was glad the cleaners hadn't thrown it out with the rest of the garbage. When he had the time, he was going to look it up and see what it was.

"Let's go," Jamal said, ushering Allie up the flagstone path.

CHAPTER NINETEEN

"I want a low cut and a neat trim on my beard. Not too much, just make it neat." Jamal trembled with excitement as he sat down in Daniel Banks's chair at Fade to Black Barber Shop.

"You got it, brother. Chauncey didn't believe you were coming in, but he said if you showed up to give you the works. It's on him, the tip and everything." Daniel Banks wrapped a paper neck strip around Jamal and threw on a black barber cape. "Come back to the sink, Jamal."

After a thorough wash of his hair and beard, Daniel directed Jamal to sit in the chair. Jamal felt the chair lower his body then lift up three stops. Daniel grabbed a black comb and a pair of scissors and started working on his hair.

Forty minutes later, Daniel passed the clippers over his head one last time, catching the stray hairs, blending, and fading the haircut into the skin. When he felt satisfied, Daniel lay Jamal back in the chair to gain access to his beard. "You said you want it shaped up, right?"

"Yeah," Jamal said, closing his eyes. Daniel opened a bottle of beard balm and massaged the liquid into Jamal's curly facial hair. This was the first time he'd visited a barber to get his beard trimmed. His father had forbidden it.

Jamal reached into his pocket. The warmth from the clay

traveled from his hand, up his arm, and into his chest. He thought about Allie's wandering hand rubbing his face as he kissed her. "On second thought, take it all off."

Daniel turned off the clippers. "What? You sure, man? Your beard is nice. It's a little scraggly around the edges, but I can fix that."

"I'm sure. I want it to be clean. For my lady."

"You're not letting Chauncey's jealous ass get to you, are you? The man talks shit about people because he's a hater." Jamal found it amusing that Chauncey's barber would be so candid about a loyal client to a total stranger. It was true, though. Chauncey was the biggest hater he'd ever met besides Tim and Renee. He made a mental note not to loosen his lips in this place.

"Nah. It's all for her. Come on, Daniel. Let's do this." Jamal leaned back and closed his eyes.

"You ain't gotta tell me more than twice." Daniel started up the clippers and got to work.

JAMAL MARVELED at feeling the wind on his face. He looked young and vibrant. "I enjoy touching you almost as much as I like the way my skin feels." He palmed the clay figurine, and it warmed his hand. "Almost as much as I enjoy touching Allie." His spine tingled, and he smiled to himself. He couldn't wait to see her reaction.

It was too early to go home. Qaylah was busy with activities at the masjid for the rest of the week. She'd asked him to do something, but he couldn't remember what it was.

It proved difficult to drive with one hand in his pocket. He plucked the statue from his pocket, careful not to sway in traffic. He held it while he rested his hand on the steering wheel. "That's better," he said.

Allie's car was at the office, as were Tim and Hannah's. Jamal entered the building and noted Hannah's stunned expression. It gave him butterflies.

She shot him a dirty look and turned away. "Sorry," Hannah said into the phone receiver. "I just lost my train of thought. Where were we?"

Jamal wondered for a moment if she were talking to his wife. He scrolled through his phone on the way to Allie's office when a heavy hand smacked him on the back.

"Yo, look who's back. Are you gonna make some phone calls to some ballers for this... house?" The look on Tim's face was priceless. "Whoa, looking good, Jamal. I can't believe you're rocking a fresh fade. And you chopped the scruff off your chin. Give me some, baby." Tim held out his hand and Jamal slapped his palm.

"Thanks, Tim."

"Chauncey is going to lose his shit when he sees you. He didn't think you would go through with it. I told him you might go because you like to look good, but I didn't expect this. You'll have all the fly honeys making appointments now."

"I'll send them your way after they buy a house from me," Jamal said, beaming. Tim's excitement got him riled up even more. He had to find her. "Yo," he said, trying to match his speech to the new look. His mother would cringe if she heard him talk that way, but he liked it. "Have you seen Allie?"

"I don't know where that waste of space is. Check her office. I'll see you tomorrow, Jamal. Be here early and we can compare notes. I want to win, Jamal. I need a better office."

"And you want to rub it in Chauncey's face?"

"You and me both," Tim said, shaking his hand again. "Alright, I'm leaving. I've got pickup games tonight with my cousins. I hope these spring thunderstorms we keep having don't ruin the fun."

"Take care." The prayer notification sounded on Jamal's phone, and he shut it off. He walked down the hall to the last office. The door opened as he raised his hand to knock.

"Jamal? Oh, my God. You shaved? I love it!"

She threw herself into his arms, and Jamal stood stiff as a board. He didn't want Hannah to see. Jamal unwrapped himself from her embrace and checked the hall. It was empty.

"Jamal, you'll never believe it. Miss Lombardi is going to close in three weeks. Isn't that insane?"

Jamal's brow furrowed. "How is that possible? Forty-five days is standard around here."

"Mister Ashraf called, and I talked to him about it. I don't know what kind of magical connection he has between lenders and the home inspectors, but he did his thing and voilà! So far, everything looks good. I have one more house to sell and I'm meeting with a couple in the morning to show it to them while the family is out."

"All of that is great news, Allie. I'm proud of you. I wish I had been the one to help you with the deal, but Ashraf owns the place for a reason."

Damn. Jamal would love to have been the one to put that look in her eyes, not to mention he wouldn't get his half of the commission now. He got screwed over long-distance by the boss. He resolved to help her sell the next one.

"Jamal?"

He went rigid at the sound of his name. Hannah rounded the corner and approached them. Instinct made him take a step back from Allie. "What is it, Hannah?" *Here we go. She's going to confront us about that kiss.*

"I'm sorry to bother you, Jamal, but can you lock up for me? I have a family emergency."

"Of course, Hannah. Is there anything I can do to help?"

"No, just lock the door. I have two sets of keys, so drop this one in the mail slot when you leave, and I'll get it in the morning."

"I will," Jamal said, accepting the keys. "I hope everything is alright."

Hannah shot him a hard glance. He stared back, waiting for her to say something.

"Thank you," she said. Hannah took a deep breath and scrunched her lips like her mouth had a nasty taste. "Goodbye, Allison."

"Goodnight, Hannah," Allie said. They watched the receptionist walk down the hall. Jamal looked after her as she turned out the lights in the waiting area before exiting from the front door.

Jamal could sense Allie's eyes watching him. He took his hand from his pocket and lay his open palm on her cheek. She mirrored the action, rubbing her small, soft hand across his face, exploring the smooth skin and the angle of his jaw where it met his chin. This was the moment they'd been waiting for.

"SHOULD we go to your office? Mine is too small." Her voice was soft and meek, but he could hear the hunger behind her words.

He responded by bending down and sweeping her into his arms. When they got to his office, she reached out and turned the door handle. He brought her to his desk and pushed aside the various stacks of contracts, notepads, and call lists.

The phone rang. He lifted the receiver and smashed it down. The heat of desire blocked his thoughts. Nothing mattered as much as this.

Allie unzipped her skirt, then arched her back, sliding the clothing off her bottom half. "I want to see all of you," Jamal insisted, fumbling with her top. He unbuttoned the blouse at last, unhooking the clasp of her bra and setting her breasts free.

His powerful need overshadowed rational thinking. Jamal claimed her lips while she undid his pants and dropped them to his ankles. A moment of doubt jerked him away from her. What was he doing? This woman was not his wife. What he was doing was haram.

"It's now or never." The words came from her mouth in a husky drawl. She traced her fingers down his torso, guiding him to her. Jamal gave in and drew her close until he found her and sunk into her. Intense satisfaction radiated throughout his body. It was too late for regret, too late to repent. He wanted her and nothing could stop him now.

"DAMN." Jamal was on the road towards home when he remembered. Katie. He was supposed to pick the little girl up from daycare. Over a dozen voicemails and text messages awaited him when he checked his cellphone. He dialed Qaylah's phone but refused to leave a voicemail. He'd have to smooth things over face-to-face.

Jamal hoped Qaylah and Katie weren't home as he drove down his street. They'd been coming home late for the past couple of weeks. What was one more night? "Fucking hell." She had illuminated the house from top to bottom.

He sat in the driveway, peppered with the smells of sweat and sex. He needed to get to the shower without running into his wife. Jamal's hand tingled against the figure inside his pocket and his fear let up. If she saw him, so what? Qaylah didn't have a sixth sense. If she did, she'd know how to keep her husband's interest.

He rubbed his thumb across the figurine, willing it to help him. *Help me evade the onslaught of this tiresome woman.* His heart was numb as he climbed out of the Escalade.

CHAPTER TWENTY

"Qaylah, I'm home." Jamal threw his keys on the entryway table as he did every night and scanned the living room and the upstairs banister. No one was in sight. On further inspection, he saw a lump of curves and lines tucked under a blanket in the living room and walked over to inspect it.

His wife lay on the sofa with a book rising and falling on her chest. *The Threat of Modern Witchcraft.* He picked up the book, scanning the blurb on the back cover and the author bio. Jamal's stomach lurched into a sickening twist. Dr. Reginald Jones-Ali. Reggie.

Did this guy have anything valuable to add to society besides hot air? Jamal scoffed as he thumbed through the book, landing on a chapter called, 'New Millennium Witches: The Business-Savvy Coven and its Social Media Infiltration.' He flipped through more pages, skimming the subtitles in each section.

Jamal laughed. "'Witches corrupting the market, cursed merchandise, tarot-infused banking, Astrological Ponzi schemes: Magical-Level-Marketing.'"

What is this guy going on about? "'Getting under your skin to get into your wallet.'" He tossed the book on the coffee table and turned to go upstairs.

"Where were you?" The groggy voice carried from underneath the rising pile of rumpled blankets. Jamal glanced over his shoulder and started, forgetting that Qaylah dyed her hair an unflattering shade of red.

"I had a busy day," he replied.

"Too busy to remember to pick up—what have you done to yourself?" She rose from the heavy bed of blankets, awake and agitated. "Jamal. Look at me."

"I'm tired, Qaylah. We can talk later." He hurried upstairs.

"I want you to look at me." Jamal heard her feet rushing across the carpeted floor and up the stairs behind him. "Show me your face. Jamal?"

He didn't bother to look back at her. There was no point. She saw what she saw, and he'd explain it later. Or he wouldn't.

"You shaved your beard? Why did you do something like that? Did something happen to it? Did you catch lice?"

"Lice?" He turned on the shower and hurried out of his clothing, dumping them on the floor. "Give me a break, Qaylah. Lice." He jumped into the shower and vigorously scrubbed his body with shower gel.

She bent to pick up his clothing. Her lips quivered as she went through his pockets, emptying the contents on the bathroom counter before placing the clothes in the laundry hamper. "I don't understand why you've done it then. You've been growing your beard since you were a teenager. Why would you do something that you know is haram?"

He jerked the curtain open and stepped out of the shower. "Have you learned any other Arabic words besides that one? 'This is haram, Jamal. That's haram Jamal.' Qaylah, sweetheart," he said, grabbing her by the wrists, "shut up and get out."

Jamal snatched his pants out of the hamper, palmed the clay figurine, then gave them to her. She looked at him with hurt in her eyes. "Did you do it because I dyed my hair?" She asked. "Are you getting back at me because you don't like my hair color?"

"Do you think everything I do concerns you? I never realized you were self-centered. Sounds narcissistic."

"You could have asked me how I felt about it, Jamal. This is a big deal. What is your family going to think? What are the people at the masjid going to say?"

"I don't give a damn what they think or say. How did you put it this morning, Qaylah? It was something about... Oh yeah. *Dominion*. You have *dominion* over your body, and I have *dominion* over mine. Now shut the fuck up and get out. You're making me waste the hot water."

Her face scrunched up, and she fled the room in tears with the pants in her hands. Jamal climbed into the hot, steamy shower and washed off the evidence of his lover.

When the water turned cold, he stepped onto the bathmat and grabbed a fresh towel to wrap around his waist and another to dry the wet curls of his fresh haircut. He brought the towel to his face to dry the hairs on his chin and laughed at his forgetfulness. The mirror reflected his new, handsome self—youthful and irresistible.

He put his love for his wife on the back burner. He felt obligated to care for her while she was pregnant and provide for their child, but he could no longer offer his heart.

With Allie by his side, he could break away from Ashraf and start his own company. They could be a team, buying and flipping houses to put on the market. They'd start off small, of course. All they needed was a stack of cash to kickstart their dreams.

Jamal went to the bedroom and opened his dresser to grab fresh clothes. Qaylah was there, sitting on the bed, waiting for him. He refused to speak. If she wanted to be a rational adult and discuss things, he would listen. If she was going to go on a tirade and tell him what a bad boy he was, she could shove it.

"I think you need to take a long, hard look in the mirror, Jamal. Your personality is off. You're not coming home on time, your clothes are different. You left Katie at the daycare, and they were threatening to kick her out of the program."

"It was an accident. They have swamped me at work for the last two weeks. I told you not to set me up at the last minute like that, didn't I?"

"She was alone. All the other children had gone home an hour before. She's three-years-old, Jamal. How could you be cruel to that little girl?"

Why didn't you call her daddy? "I wasn't cruel to her, Qaylah. I was getting work done. How else do you expect the bills to get paid?"

"Is that what this is about? Money?"

"No, it's not about money. I'm sorry you had to hire a driver to swing by to pick up your little one on the way to the masjid. I made a mistake, okay?"

"I didn't hire a car to pick her up. I took the bus to my doctor's appointment then went to the masjid as scheduled."

"You took the bus all the way to her daycare?"

"No. I called Brian, and he said he'd be happy to get her."

If looks could kill. Jamal's body went rigid. "What did you say?" Jamal put the figurine on his dresser and stepped into a pair of underwear. "You called Brian?"

"That's right."

"How'd you get his number?"

"He gave it to me. It was in the envelope with the money.

He told me to use it whenever I needed something. Today, I needed him, and he was there for me."

"Good for him. Did he come inside the house or just drop her off?"

"Why does that matter?"

"Did he come inside the house?"

"I knew it. You're jealous. You can't be reasonable. I called him to pick up his daughter, who you neglected to care for. She has a right to be taken care of by you—you're her stepfather in case you've forgotten."

"You're not allowed to see him again as long as you're living under my roof."

"What did you say?"

"You heard me."

"Do you think I'm a child, Jamal? How dare you?"

"If you do, there'll be consequences," he said.

"Mama, Mama, why are you yelling?" Katie stood in the doorway with Mister Sniffles tucked under her arm.

"Go back to bed, Katie. I'm talking to your mother." Jamal towered over the young girl, and she shrank from him. "What's your problem? Stop acting like I'm the bad guy."

He took a step towards her, and she shrieked. She turned to run, and on her way out, bumped into the dresser. The figurine fell off the dresser. All but the head shattered.

"You little bitch, you broke it!" Jamal scooped up the head and lunged for the girl.

"Mama!"

"Get away from her." Qaylah side-swiped him with her full weight, knocking him off balance. They tumbled to the floor. Qaylah recovered, picked up her daughter and walked her to the child's bedroom. The door slammed in Jamal's face. She clicked the lock that Jamal neglected to remove although he had promised.

"Qaylah," come out here, right now. "I said open this door." He banged on it until the heavy wood left his palm bright red.

"Leave us alone, you devil!" He heard their sobs on the other side of the door and backed away from it. Why was he trying so hard?

Jamal got dressed and packed an overnight bag. He grabbed a suit bag from the closet, shoes, and toiletries, and pocketed his keys. If those bitches didn't want him here, he wouldn't beg to stay. He had other options anyway.

He trudged down the stairs with his clothes and went to the kitchen. Jamal opened the desk drawer in the study nook and opened the file box in the back, where Qaylah kept important documents. The manilla envelope full of cash was there. *Predictable and boring as ever.* He dropped it into his bag and left the house.

A sharp piece of clay dug into his thigh through the fabric of his jogging pants, but he didn't mind. He felt better knowing it was with him. Jamal got on the highway and headed towards The Papyrus Hotel. He could use a little five-star service. Jamal reached into the bag and squeezed the fat envelope between his fingers. He left the house because Qaylah told him to, and she was going to foot the bill.

CHAPTER TWENTY-
ONE

JAMAL SLEPT through the morning prayer. He checked his messages and muted Qaylah's phone number when he woke up. After a good night's sleep on the king-sized bed with its cool Egyptian cotton sheets and lofty duvet, he found it difficult to get his day started. This was the vacation he'd been longing for. The high-powered shower hit his body from three directions, washing away the minute traces of marital guilt.

Before breakfast, Jamal enjoyed his first shave with hot-towel service. He smiled at himself in the mirror afterwards and hoped Allie realized what a catch he was. He stuffed himself, gorging on a huge breakfast of eggs, waffles, home fries, and coffee. None of that half-assed burnt shit that Qaylah slung on the plates today.

He flirted with the female server who brought his food to the room. She slipped him her number on the way out. He added it to his phone, wondering if she'd be willing to join him tonight when Allie came over. Allie didn't seem like the type to mind company. He pondered the delicious possibilities.

The office was already full when he arrived. "Good morning, Hannah. How are you?" Jamal flashed her a smile but knew better than to waste precious moments waiting for the receptionist to thaw. She was too intent on staring him down.

"Jamal, what's happening?" Chauncey walked past him on his way from the break room. "You did it. You went to David, right? I can't believe it. You look like a normal person now."

"No, he doesn't. He looked better with a beard." Renee stood in the break room's doorway holding a plate with a breakfast burrito and fruit in one hand, and coffee in the other.

"I didn't ask for your opinion," Jamal said.

"Too bad. I think you could use my help. Your numbers are abysmal, Jamal. You've lost your touch."

"The last thing I need is your concern, Renee. You don't know shit about real estate."

"What the fuck are you talking about, Jamal? I'm here, aren't I?"

"You're nothing but a third-rate coattail rider," Jamal said. "You barely passed the exam. Ashraf gave you a job because your ghetto-ass mother used to scrub his toilets."

"Damn, Jamal. That's a low blow," Chauncey said.

Renee scowled. "Scrubbing toilets doesn't make a Black woman ghetto. It's wrong to speak ill of the dead. You should apologize."

"I don't think so," Jamal said.

"Does your mama know you hate Black women?" Renee asked.

"Fuck you." Jamal left them standing there in utter astonishment. The clay figurine burned against his thigh.

"THERE YOU ARE, Allie. I've been searching for you." Jamal strode into one of the smaller conference rooms where Allie sat with Tim. He pulled up a chair and dropped his messenger bag on the table before he sat down.

Tim jumped away from Allie like he'd been making a move

on her. Jamal didn't take offense. Everything in this office was a competition.

"Hi, Jamal. You're here early. Any news on the murder house?"

"Good one, Tim. Why don't we get together this afternoon to talk about leads?" Tim was impossible any time of the day, but his antics wouldn't spoil his mood today. Jamal had too much important stuff to discuss with Allie.

"Sure. I might convince a friend of my uncle to buy the condo. He lives in Singapore. The problem is, it might take a while before he agrees to come and see it. I think we can pencil him in for now."

"Ran out of uncles and aunts? It's good that you're branching out," Jamal said.

Tim held up his hands. "I can see when I'm not wanted. Let's meet up at two o'clock, okay?"

"Fine. Close the door on your way out." Tim shot a glance at Allie, then back to Jamal before leaving.

Allie smoothed the wrinkles out of her skirt. "Is something on your mind?"

Jamal grinned, stretching his mouth until it threatened to crack open at the corners. "A lot is on my mind, Allie." He sprang out of his chair, closed the blinds, locked the door, then reached into his pants pocket to rub the broken idol for good luck. The warmth of the clay calmed him, and he settled down.

"Like what?" She asked. Her body language seemed odd. Jamal figured she wasn't a morning person and left it at that.

"I have a solution for buying back your house."

Allie dropped her hands into her lap. "I'm listening."

"Baby, I've got enough money to help you buy your house and to invest in another one. We are going to secure our future, right here, right now."

"What are you talking about, Jamal?"

He reached into his messenger bag and pulled out the manilla envelope, holding it open for her to see. "It's all right here. I've got plenty of money to help us get started. This is just a taste of what I can get my hands on."

Allie's eyes widened, and a smile broke out on her face. "How did you come up with so much money? You didn't do anything illegal, did you?"

"Nope. This is family money, inherited a couple of days ago. I need to invest it in something, and I thought, why not buy a cheap house, fix it up and flip it, then buy a bigger house, and then, an even bigger house until we can start our own realtor business?"

"We?"

"Yes. We, Allie. I want us to do this together. First, I want to get your house back for you."

Allie threw her arms around Jamal's neck, burying him in the silk of her hair. "Oh, God, you are the most beautiful man. But I can't let you do this for me, Jamal. I wouldn't feel right if you gave me so much money."

"Are you kidding me? Allie, you have changed my world in such a short time. I'm free because of you. Helping you is the least I can do if we're going to be together."

"Jamal, I told you before. I'm not interested in settling down. It's not something I aspire to do."

"Last night was magical, and I know that I can't live without you. I don't care about marriage, Allie. We'll do it your way. Please, take this." He reached into his bag for a second envelope and filled it with twenty-thousand dollars from Qaylah's stash.

"Why are you carrying this much cash? A cashier's check would be wise," she said, staring at the envelope like it was going to bite her. "Are you sure you gained this by legal means?"

"Yes. I inherited it from my family, and now I'd like to invest it in real estate. I plan to get an attorney and accountant to take care of it for us. In the meantime, some of it will serve as collateral for a bank loan, and then I'll scout houses until I find the perfect one."

His eyes lit up as he told her his plan.

"If you're feeling charitable, you can buy the other house that I've got on the market," she said.

Jamal's face brightened. "That's a good idea." He leaned over and kissed her lips.

"Jamal, I was kidding. Don't do that."

"Why not? It fits in with our plans. It's a sound investment."

"I feel funny about it."

"It's not marriage."

"But it's an enormous commitment. I don't know if I can handle being indebted to someone like that."

Jamal laughed and took her head in his hands. "Don't be crazy, girl. If anyone is indebted, it's me. I can't get enough of you. I'm here for you, however you need me."

Allie removed his hands from her face and got out of her chair. She paced back and forth, staring into the neglected gravel pit behind the rental office where a new subdivision waited to be built for the last six months.

"Let me think about it. Taking this kind of money from someone I'm close to is a big deal. You and I are strangers."

Jamal walked to her and put his arms around her waist from behind. "We're not strangers. I've been inside you. We may not know the little things, but there is no greater knowing than what we've done."

"That's sweet, Jamal. We had sex on your desk, but it didn't cure cancer. It's not a big deal. We're not lovers. We're not even friends. You and I are co-workers and total strangers."

She peeled his hands from around her waist. "I've taken advantage of you. Take the money back and we'll keep things professional from now on."

"Allie, I'm a grown man who knows what he wants. And right now, I know I need you in my life, and I want you to take this money and go after what belongs to you." He picked up the envelope and put it in her hand. "Please. I won't be able to sleep at night if you don't take it."

Allie looked down at the envelope. "How about I keep it in the safe at my apartment? Then I can give it back when you realize what a mistake you've made."

The corners of Jamal's mouth turned upward in triumph. "Do whatever you want."

CHAPTER TWENTY-TWO

JAMAL CALLED potential buyers and set up appointments for the condo. By late afternoon, he'd been out longer than expected. He called off the meeting with Tim.

It was just as well. Tim wanted Jamal to look stupid when the time came for a buyer to sign on the dotted line. Jamal would split the commission with him, but there was no way he was going to be second fiddle to that jerk. The buyer, of course, would come from Jamal's connections, not the Chang family tree or their friends.

The sky turned brownish green, congested with clouds. The branches of the old willow tree bore the same color as the sky, weighed down and listless by the oppressive humidity.

Jamal reached into the back seat and pulled out a small package. He got out of the car and unhooked his old sign from the post, dropping it on the ground. Water droplets splashed in his eyes and ran down the side of his face as he hung the new one with his beardless, beaming face. *Lady Killer.*

The skies opened, and he felt heavier drops fall on his head and shoulders. The air was thick with the smell of honeysuckle and tender leaves on the azaleas. Jamal put his head back, feeling the sprinkles tickle his cheeks as it ran down his chin to his throat. He picked up the old sign and tossed it into the garbage bin at the curb.

It was a lot of cash to deal with, despite giving Allie one-fourth of it. Banks would ask too many questions about its origin, and he didn't want the hassle of splitting it up and leaving a paper trail for now. He hastened to secure the sign and get inside the house out of the rain.

It looked like tornado weather. He reached into his pocket to warm his fingers against the jagged clay figurine and got an idea.

Jamal sheltered on the porch and stared at the willow tree. Under the circumstances, the house was going to take time to sell with the terrible publicity about Tobias. The news of a dead dog in the dryer was bound to make it into the newspapers as well. Rosewood Hollow was a small city, and news traveled fast.

It would be safe here for a little while. Even if he found a buyer, they weren't bound to move in for at least a month or two. He could stall them while he found the perfect place for the money.

He unlocked the house and placed the messenger bag on the floor in the living room, grabbed the money, then went out back to the shed. He took down a shovel hanging from the pegboard and rolled up his sleeves.

After some time, he finished digging a watery hole large enough to hide the money at the base of the willow tree. He wrapped his new nest egg in a large freezer bag, minus five thousand dollars for expenses, namely, a new dryer and more nights at the Papyrus Hotel.

Once he covered the money bag with soggy shovelfuls of earth, he tamped it down and replaced the top layer of grass. By now, his shirt had soaked through. He used the hose in the backyard to wash the shovel, then put it back inside the shed.

you come with me for a second? I need to show you something."

Sighing, Officer Macklin looked him over. "Alright, you've got five minutes and then I need to get on the highway to beat the traffic. I hate driving when the sky turns green. Tornadoes."

"It won't take long, I promise."

She followed him across the parking lot, and he flung open the passenger door behind the driver's seat. Buck opened his eyes and sniffed the air, then went back to sleep.

Officer Macklin peered inside. "Buck?" The dog responded to his name, wagging his tail, and stretching. She shut the door and frowned. "It's him alright. That creates lots of questions, Mister Jackson. For starters, where has he been?"

"How should I know?"

"Well, he's in your car," she said, adjusting her umbrella.

"He ran up to me when I was at the house. I don't know where he was before that." Buck barked and tapped his feet on the glass. "Get off my seat," Jamal said.

"This is strange," Officer Macklin said.

"Do you think someone wanted Tobias to believe Buck was in the dryer?" Jamal asked.

"Are you saying someone filled the dryer with a black rug and pig's blood, hoping Tobias would kill himself?"

"What?"

"Yes. Someone pulled an elaborate prank, Mister Jackson, but like you've speculated, I don't think they did it for laughs. You buy rugs to stage your homes, don't you?"

Jamal raised an eyebrow. "You don't think I had something to do with it, do you?"

"You told me yourself that you didn't get along."

"That was annoying neighbor stuff, not..."

"Manslaughter? Listen, Mister Jackson, I'm sure you're not involved, but I have to ask the questions, don't I?"

"Yeah, I guess so." Jamal tugged at his collar. He hadn't expected her to turn the tables like she had. Manslaughter? Buck whimpered to be let out of the S.U.V. "What should we do with him?"

"I'll take him into the station. We can run tests on his fur to see if it's possible to tell where he's been or who he's been with."

"You can do that?"

Officer Macklin smiled. "Didn't Officer Parker tell you? Us forensics folks learned our tricks from *CSI* like everybody else. But we have cooler equipment."

She opened the door, and Buck climbed out of the vehicle. He growled at Jamal. "That's enough of that, Buck," she said in a firm voice. The dog tucked his tail and waited. "See? You've got to be firm with him. He's never bitten me."

"Congratulations. I'm sure he'll be happier with you than he is with me," Jamal said, nursing a bite on his forearm.

"Ooh, that's nasty. Do you have something to clean it?"

"I'll be fine."

"Are you sure? Buck has bitten his fair share of people. Oh, that reminds me. I talked to my mother about the Frauenhaus family. Mama used to do domestic work for them. She loved that house. If she could afford it, she would have snatched it up for herself."

"Really? I'll give her a good deal if she wants it."

"Ha. It's out of her budget. Although Tobias's suicide certainly ought to bring down the price."

"We could work something out," he said.

"Nah. In the old days, the house extended from the willow tree all the way to the end of the house Tobias lived in. Mama would want the property in its entirety, which is definitely out of her budget." Officer Macklin looked thoughtful for a moment, like she might make him an offer. If she had, Jamal would have taken it.

"What did your mother have to say about the family?"

"That they were into witchcraft. It was their custom to allow only one man to live in the home."

"Why just one?"

"Too many males on the property blocked their energy or something. Whenever a member of the house gave birth to a male infant, they turned him over to the state. They kept all of the girls though. Mama said her friend who worked at the old Copperhead Cliffs Orphanage remembered that there were seven boys brought in during the late eighties."

"Nobody did anything to stop it?"

"Like what? People minded their business. They cared for the girls and sent the boys to loving homes. What was there to stop?"

Officer Macklin adjusted the umbrella to share it with Jamal as they walked Buck towards the station.

"Anyway, April Rucker was the one who started all the trouble. She married Curtis Tandy in secret and sneaked him into the house. Things started going south for the family quickly. They fell into financial straits and had to let Mama go, along with the nanny and the cook. Sometime later, they discovered Curtis living in an old bricked up apartment above April's room."

"What happened?"

"The matriarch Alexandra murdered them for breaking the family covenant."

"Just for bringing a boy into the home?" Jamal asked.

"Rules are rules, I guess. The police came and arrested Alexandra and a few others who defended her. Eventually, the remaining women sold half the land to Tobias after he came back from God knows where. He claimed it was his birthright and demanded they turn over the rest. That's when the feuding and lawsuits started."

"What happened to the rest of the family?"

"I don't know. Without Alexandra, the remaining women couldn't hold it together. Mama said one of the last women who owned the house couldn't afford property taxes. The bank came in and took it from her. She died on the spot when they did it. Hanged herself from the big willow tree. She was April's sister. Her name was Tomeeka. Her daughter made a promise to get it back one day. You alright?"

He swallowed and his heart skipped a beat. "I think I've been seeing her ghost."

"Maybe. Some old houses have lots of ghosts."

"The daughter... Is she looking to buy back the house? What's her contact information? I'd like to speak with her."

"I don't think so, Mister Jackson. They need to move on."

"Are you serious? Why are you making decisions for them?"

"It's like I said. There have been lots of ghosts. I don't think it's right to unbury the past."

"Then I guess I'll have to go around you." He'd have to look up the surviving family and see if they wanted to talk business.

"Her daughter took it hard. If I were you, I wouldn't interfere with those women. They need to heal."

The rain picked up as they stepped under the shelter of the police station's entrance. Buck shook water from his coat and sat down.

Officer Macklin reached into her purse. "Anyway, here's my card. If you see anything else or have more information about the dog, call me. In the meantime, I'm going to take this fella inside. Let's go, Buck."

Buck stood and wagged his tail. He seemed in good spirits with Officer Macklin, but he growled at Jamal again.

"Calm down, mutt. Be glad someone is here to take care of you," Jamal said.

"I don't know why he acts that way towards you. I've never seen him be mean except to cats."

Jamal watched the police officer and the orphaned dog enter the building. *Gatekeeping bitch. Good riddance to both of them.* He felt better knowing he'd never see the mutt again, but there were many unanswered questions. Why was Officer Macklin getting in his way? Who would go to such lengths to fake the dog's death? A crazy person, that's who. Maybe a crazy daughter who wanted her house back.

His phone rang. He answered it without thinking. "Hello?"

"As Salaamu Alaikum, Jamal. This is your mother."

"What's up?"

"'What's up?' What do you mean by that? You can't return my greeting properly?"

"I'm in a hurry. Tell me what you need."

"What's gotten into you? Qaylah said you were acting strangely. Why is she at my house in tears? What did you do to her and that precious little girl?"

"What goes on between a man and his wife is his business," he said, clenching his jaw.

"I think you should come over here and speak to me and your father, Jamal. I don't appreciate–"

Jamal tapped the screen, ending the call. He blocked his mother when she called back. Time was wasting. The Rosewood Hollow Clerk's Office closed its doors in about twenty minutes. He was going to find the daughter and tell her to buy the damned house.

CHAPTER TWENTY-
THREE

"No, Sir. I don't recall a woman named Alexandra Rucker owning a house on Spiegel Road. I'm unfamiliar with the last name." The woman behind the counter at the Rosewood Hollow Genealogical Society sniffed from her wide nostrils and clutched the odd-looking flannel bag around her neck.

Jamal couldn't find any information at the clerk's office. The records were missing from the online files, and no one seemed able to help him. A resourceful clerk directed him to the genealogical society.

The woman removed her hand from the pouch hanging around her neck when she caught Jamal watching. He tried guessing her age, but her youthful black face and contrasting stark white bangs made it difficult.

"Are you sure? They called it Frauenhaus. Can you check under that name?"

"Sorry. I can't help you." She picked up his card and handed it to him.

"Keep it, it's yours," Jamal said.

"I'm alright," the woman said, picking it up and thrusting it out to him.

"Thanks anyway." Jamal snatched it from her hand and shoved it into his pant pocket, next to the comforting heat coming from the tiny clay bulge. He let his hand linger on it while the woman pursed her lips and turned her back to him.

"If you'll excuse me, I have books to shelve." Her heels clicked in an irregular rhythm from a slight limp as she walked away with an armload of books on the polished marble floor.

Weirdo. He rubbed his left eye and wondered if he was developing an allergy. He saw through it with some difficulty, seemingly from behind a white, cloudy film. The fresh-cut lavender in the room reminded him of a venue for old ladies to attend tea parties and play bridge. The scent gave him a headache.

As Jamal turned to leave, a deep voice caught him off guard. "Don't mind Lisa, she's been in a bad mood for most of her life," the man said. Jamal turned and saw a barrel-chested man thrusting his hand out at him. "Moses Reneau, historian."

"Jamal Jackson." Jamal shook the man's dark, manicured hand. There was an extreme contrast between his clean, well-kept nails and busted, swollen knuckles.

"My mama told me that girls don't like it if your nails are dirty. My daddy said if I came home crying, he would give me something to cry about," Moses said, rubbing his knobby joints. "I listened to them both. Thank God, he taught me to box. Pretty girls and fighting go hand in hand."

"You box?"

"Underground, bare-knuckle. You can see how shredded my hands have gotten. If you're interested, I'll give you the details."

"I wish I could. I need this pretty face to sell houses," Jamal said.

"I understand."

"Almost done, Moses," the strange woman said, gathering more books.

"Take your time, Lisa," Moses said.

"I guess pretty is subjective," Jamal said.

"Every woman is pretty in her own way. Even the ugly ones," Moses said. They watched her disappear into one room and emerge from another adjoining one.

"I think she hates men or something."

"Nah. Lisa hates everybody. I overheard you telling her you wanted information about Frauenhaus."

"Have you heard of it?"

"I have."

"What can you tell me about it?"

"That anybody dealing with that place is looking for trouble."

"You're right. But what if I said I need to figure out how to get out of trouble?"

"Stay away from that land and you'll be fine."

"Can't do that. I sell houses, and I won't leave it alone until it's out of my hands and into a buyer's."

Moses looked over his shoulder. "Then you'd better come with me."

MOSES LED Jamal to the kitchen area at the back of the building and opened what looked like an ordinary pantry door. He knocked on the wall, opening a hidden panel behind which was a dark, airy space.

"This way."

"What's in there?" Jamal had come here seeking answers, not more mysteries.

"All the information you're looking for and then some," Moses said. He took out a handkerchief from his pocket and reached inside the dark space. Jamal heard the flick of a light switch and the dark area beyond the panel lit up in shades of amber, revealing a winding marble staircase. Moses slid open a glass door and gestured for Jamal to step inside.

"I bet there's an interesting story about this secret passage," Jamal said.

Moses smiled. "It's not a secret. Anyone can enter with permission. Shall we find out about your house?"

Jamal wondered what he was getting into, but he'd come here of his own volition. "Alright. If you think you can find something, I'd appreciate it."

"I know I can. This way, please."

Moses closed the door behind them, then walked down the steps. The air was heavy with the scent of lavender and roses. As they descended, it became strong enough to make him dizzy.

As Jamal's eyes adjusted to the dark, they jumped out of focus again. He held onto the rail with one hand and rubbed at them with the other. It didn't help.

They reached the next level and Moses led Jamal down an opening between hundreds of bookshelves. Jamal stayed close as Moses, adept and confident, snaked between rows adorned with cryptic markings, not stopping to verify his location.

Jamal took in the big man's fashionable but quirky style. He admired the way he moved with confidence in the eye-catching outfit. Jamal wouldn't be caught dead in a mint jacket with navy slacks, no socks, and cognac loafers. But it worked for Moses, contrasting attractively with his dark complexion.

Moses stopped deep inside the stacks of books and pointed at his feet. "Watch your step. There's damage on the floor right here," he said, tapping his foot. "This is the vault, as we call it. Any information you need on a location or a person within the Tri-City area is here."

"I'm impressed," Jamal said. "How far down does the vault

go?" He leaned over the banister, counting the lower staircases, but they descended into darkness.

"I'm permitted to go six floors down, but there's a lot more than that. I'm told that the society can reach back to the motherland before the Spanish and Portuguese even thought about enslaving us. Here we are. Spiegel Road, Frauenhaus Estate." Moses ran his finger along the ledge of a shelf, showing Jamal a set of gold and black volumes.

"How did you gain access to all this information?"

"Donations, loans, forceful acquisitions," he said, shrugging. "The same way the government does."

Jamal raised an eyebrow, but the gleam in Moses' eyes made it unclear if he was serious.

"It's impressive, but I hope we don't stay long. My eyes are seeing double." Jamal stepped back from the banister and leaned against a chair at a small study table. It bumped the table, teetering a banker's lamp.

"What do you need to know about the place?" Moses asked.

"Who recently owned the house?"

"The Rucker's owned it until Alexandra killed April. After that, I believe it passed through the hands of several cousins."

"Legitimate sales on the books?"

"Let's look." Moses grabbed three books and took them to the table. He flipped through several pages, switched books, and flipped some more.

"I need to know who owned it when it went into foreclosure. I think she might be sabotaging the sale of the house."

"Why do you think that?" Moses closed the book and flipped through the third one.

"Because strange things have happened."

"Like what?"

"Six hundred dead birds on the lawn. Strange symbols

painted on the door, and some other stuff." Far worse things, like a neighbor blowing out his own brains.

"First, what the hell? And second, what do you mean, 'six hundred dead birds on the lawn?'"

Jamal squeezed his eyes shut. "It's preposterous and complicated. But someone is keeping me from selling this house, and I have to figure out who it is."

"Maybe the best thing to do is not sell the house," Moses said, switching back to the first book.

"It's like I told you before. I'm a real estate agent. It's what I came to do, and I'm not leaving until it's done. Do you think Alexandra's daughter would sabotage me?"

"Without a doubt, I can say she wouldn't."

"How can you be so sure?"

"Because she's been dead for twelve years." Moses thrust a book at Jamal. "She worked hard putting food on the table for her children. Eventually, she snapped. They put her in Dominion Springs for evaluation. When she got out, she hanged herself from that big willow tree on the front lawn."

Jamal studied the open page. It was a photocopy of a death certificate. "Marlene Rucker, death by suicide, age thirty-one."

There went his lead. "I was told she vowed to buy back the house."

"I knew Marlene. When her sister April died, she had what I'd call a temporary mental break. She stayed at Dominion Springs for a few months, then got on with her life. Regrettably, she didn't live long. I suspect there was a lot going on in that house."

"There were more women living there. Do you know what happened to them?"

"That I can't tell you," Moses said.

Jamal looked puzzled. "Why not?"

"Because someone has been here before us, ripping out

pages." Moses showed him where someone had torn several pages from all three volumes. "I'll need to report this first thing in the morning. Give me your number and I'll let you know what I find out in the database."

"Can't you look now?"

"I'm sorry. We closed about twenty minutes ago. I need to lock up."

"Thanks for your help. I'll find my way out," Jamal said, not hiding his irritation. He stepped around the table, but Moses blocked him.

"I need to ask you something before you go. How long have you had your condition?"

"I don't have a condition," Jamal said, shaking his head.

"It's just that the moment I saw you, I noticed your eyes."

"I must have gotten some dust in them earlier." *Or dirt from burying the money.* Buck had thrown a wrench into his plans, and he hadn't found time to shower.

"You've got more than dust in your eyes, friend. I don't know if you're a believer in black magic, but someone's gotten hold of your person. Your eyes have scales on them."

"Scales? What is that a metaphor?"

"Nope. I'm being literal." Moses walked over to Jamal and grabbed him by the shoulders. "Come here, I'll show you." He marched Jamal to a large mirror hanging on a wall next to the banister. "The light down here is dim, but you can see there's a slight film covering your eyes."

Jamal glanced from Moses to the mirror, then approached it with caution. He gasped. A thin white membrane covered his eyes like a pair of contact lenses.

"Priests say one sign of possession is cloudy eyes."

"Maybe it's cataracts."

"You had a problem with your vision before today?"

"Not exactly." He gripped the clay figure in his pocket but found it cold and unresponsive.

"Her power is useless here, Jamal. She can't comfort you right now." Moses laid a hand on Jamal's shoulder, causing him to flinch.

"What are you talking about? Whose power?"

"I saw you reaching into your pocket several times. Is that where you're keeping it?"

"Keeping what?"

"They call it, 'Die Frau,'" Moses said, flipping through one of the damaged books. "See?" He showed Jamal a drawing of the figure he had in his pocket. "She's the goddess of the Frauenhaus witches. They practiced witchcraft in the back-woods of Rosewood Hollow in the early eighteen hundreds. Only a powerful family could do something like that in Bible country."

Jamal frowned. "I didn't come here for a history lesson. Unless you can tell me who's fucking with the house, I'm done."

"Admit that something has happened to you, and I'll help you get rid of it."

"Nothing's wrong with me, and I'm leaving now, or you're gonna face your next opponent."

"Jamal. Do you believe in God?"

He hesitated. "That's none of your business."

"Who are you turning your back on, brother? Jesus? Jeho-vah? Allah?"

Jamal flinched. "I'm agnostic."

"Bullshit. You're a good boy gone wrong. I can see it on your face. You need to let this go, man. Get away from that house before something happens that you can't undo."

"Fuck off." Jamal walked towards the staircase.

"*A'udhu Billahi min ash shaytaan ir rajeem...*" Moses said

the phrase and blew air onto the back of Jamal's neck. He halted and turned towards Moses with pure hatred in his eyes.

"Stop it. Don't do that!"

Moses repeated the phrase in painstaking Arabic, but the words had an immediate effect on Jamal.

Beads of sweat broke out on his forehead as stabbing pains attacked him from behind his eyelids. Moses' sloppy but effective recitation poked at the devil inside Jamal. He reached out and grabbed Moses' wrist with enough force to bring the big man down to his knees.

"I said, stop." A much deeper, distorted voice came from Jamal's throat.

"Let me go before you break my wrist," Moses said.

"Maybe I should rip your whole arm off."

"That's enough." Jamal turned. Lisa stood at the bottom of the staircase. "Let him go. Now."

"Shut up, you ugly bitch." He turned back to Moses. Lisa's swift feet glided across the floor towards the men. A hard knock to the head sent Jamal onto the floor next to Moses. The last thing he saw before losing consciousness was a shock of white hair and her angry face.

CHAPTER TWENTY-FOUR

"WHAT WERE YOU THINKING, taking him downstairs by yourself? It's clear that he's troubled."

"I wanted to help him."

"It was stupid, Moses. This isn't our business."

"Lisa, he's out of his depth. I don't think he has any idea what's happened to him."

Jamal listened to the conversation. He couldn't move or speak, and his head throbbed.

"I think he's waking up. If he acts like a fool again, I'll put him in a coma."

"You didn't have to go gangster on the man, hitting him like that. I had it under control."

"Give me a break, Moses. You're not even Muslim, nor do you know Arabic. What kind of exorcism were you gonna do?"

"I saw it online in a video. He seemed to respond to it," Moses said. His voice was devoid of the confidence he had earlier.

"He responded alright. As big as you are, Moses, he had you on your knees begging. What would you have done if I didn't come in?"

Jamal listened to the silence in the room.

"Well?"

"I don't know, Lisa. I wasn't thinking."

"You can't help him if he doesn't want it. Send him away."

"Okay. If it makes you happy." Jamal heard the distinct sound of lips smacking together. He frowned and his eyelids fluttered.

"He's waking up," Lisa said.

"I can take it from here," Moses said.

"Are you sure, Moses?"

"Yes, Lisa. If I need you, I'll shout." Jamal listened as Lisa walked past him and up a set of creaky stairs.

"Jamal. Wake up, man. Jamal?" Moses gave him a gentle shake to rouse him out of his stillness.

Jamal's eyes opened and stared up at the blurry ceiling. He couldn't move his head.

"Possession wreaks havoc on the body," Moses said, placing his hands on the sides of Jamal's head and rotating it back and forth. "It saps the strength, fouls the mood and body, and changes personalities. You may have noticed an increase in your libido or a propensity to harm others. If you don't get this taken care of, it will get worse." Moses let go of his head and shined a light in his eyes.

"You were kissing her."

"Sorry?"

"Lisa. I told you she was ugly, and you brushed it off."

Moses laughed. "Man, if you think she's ugly, that's one less cat for me to worry about. I'm crazy about that woman, crooked nose, and all."

"You two live together?"

"That's right."

"What did she do to me?"

"She bopped you on the head with her magic stick."

"What?"

Moses picked up a wooden walking stick. "She bought it in

Ghana on our honeymoon. Takes it everywhere. She wasn't trying to harm you, but you left her no choice."

"She's your wife?"

"It'll be fifteen years in December. Don't worry about the knot on the back of your head. You'll be right as rain in about twenty minutes." Moses dabbed at Jamal's forehead with a wet cloth. "Until then, I'm going to gather copies of everything I have about the house, free of charge."

JAMAL TURNED his head and studied his surroundings. He was lying on a pull-out sofa in a vintage-style living room, circa 1940s. He closed his eyes again, waiting for the pain to subside.

"Good morning, Jamal. I guess it took longer than twenty minutes. I hope the couch didn't wreck your back last night."

Bemused, Jamal looked at Moses, who wore a deep turquoise button-down shirt with a tweed vest and navy slacks.

"Bon appétit." He set down a tray of pancakes, fruit, and a glass of orange juice next to a mug of steaming coffee.

"I was here all night?" Jamal's stomach rumbled. He hadn't eaten since yesterday morning.

"You passed out."

Jamal used Moses's hand to sit up and stretched his weary muscles. "I'd hate to see what Lisa does when she wants to harm someone."

"She was protecting me. Whatever has a hold on you strengthens you. Or, perhaps I should say, whoever has a hold."

"You think somebody is possessing me with black magic? Wouldn't I be able to tell?"

"It depends. Have you tried to pray in the past few days? Do you notice anything strange happening in your house?"

"Like what?"

"Cold air, tapping in the walls, voices. There are several things that would signal a disturbance." Moses moved the tray closer to Jamal and sat down in an armchair facing the couch.

Jamal lifted the coffee cup to his lips and swallowed the hot liquid. Heat scalded his esophagus and settled in the empty pit of his stomach. The headache he nursed went into submission and his heart fluttered inside his chest, coming back to life with the aid of the caffeine.

"I had a lot of strange dreams last night." He reached into his pocket for the clay figure. His heartbeat accelerated.

"There's no need to panic, Jamal. I took it out of your pocket. It's there on the table in the box," Moses said, pointing.

Jamal ripped the top off the box, spilling droplets of coffee on his foot. The broken head, with jagged terracotta slivers where the neck should be, lay in the box like he said.

"Die Frau," Moses said, sliding a photograph across the table from a file folder. "If you look at this picture, you can see the house in its original form. It sits between two giant willow trees and several small ones, on which there are markings... initials, love hearts, and this." He showed Jamal a second photograph.

"There's a carving on the tree," Jamal said, leaning forward. It was difficult to see through the layers of white swirly matter covering his eyes, but it was there. "The figurine."

"They carved it into both of the giant trees. I never noticed." Jamal looked closer. The second largest willow tree sat at the edge of the property line, on Tobias's side.

"Look at the children in this photograph. See what they're holding?" A group of teenage girls stood next to the willow tree where Jamal had buried the money.

"They all have them?"

"Yes, just like the one you're clinging to. It's easier to spread the faith when you have a tangible representative. It's a token," Moses said, pointing to the remnants of the one in Jamal's hand. "Look at how attached you are to it. You only let it go when you were unconscious. You're like a baby with a pacifier. I can't force you, but for your sake, leave it in the box."

Jamal squeezed it in his palm until he left a deep impression. "Let's say, for the sake of argument, that I am possessed. How did it happen, and what would I do to fix it?"

"You could try ruqya. I'm assuming as a Muslim you've heard of it?"

"Yes, of course. You're suggesting that I get an exorcism."

"Absolutely. If you start now, you can save yourself years of agony. If you don't seek help, it will be more difficult to tame it in the future."

"It?"

"Whatever jinn or spirit is violating your person. You need a professional to get it out of you."

"Can't you help me? You seem knowledgeable about the subject."

"No, friend, I can't help you. I'm not even Muslim."

"But you know a lot about it. You recited a supplication in the library. We learned different prayers as a kid, but I never knew they could hurt like that. Never believed it."

"Yeah," Moses said with a sheepish grin. "I overheard my cousin Rukhsana once. I gave you all I had. If you truly want help, she's the one you need to call." Moses reached for a pen and paper and scribbled a name and number on it, then handed it to Jamal.

"Rukhsana Davis, registered nurse, certified in hijama." A cloud of unease settled over Jamal as he read the information.

"I believe that's cupping, correct?"

"Yeah. This address is in Salem, Virginia."

"She moved to Rosewood Hollow a few months ago, but

Now that the money was secure, he could focus on the task at hand: selling this house once and for all, barring no more unsettling events. He placed a hand on the banister of the front porch to climb it and stopped dead in his tracks.

"What the actual fuck?" Buck sat on the flagstone path, staring at him.

～

"Is Officer Parker in the station? I need to talk to him. It's urgent." Jamal sat in the parking lot at the Rosewood Hollow Police Station, talking on the phone to a dispatcher. Buck lay on the floor, sleeping. The fucker had bitten him, and he didn't dare leave the dog unattended for the sake of his Cadillac's interior.

Buck was alive. Someone hated Tobias enough to stage the dog's death. Someone without a conscience.

"He's on vacation," the dispatcher said. "I can call another officer if you'd like."

Jamal spotted a woman with red locs styled in a bun, holding a black and white polka-dotted umbrella. He bolted out of the Escalade and slammed the door. "Officer Macklin, wait up." Jamal caught up with her before she could climb into her beat-up blue sedan.

"Hi, how can I help you?" Officer Macklin kept one hand on the door handle and the other on her umbrella, searching his face for recognition.

"Jamal Jackson. We met at Spiegel Road," he said.

"That's right. You're the real estate guy. You look different shaved. I liked it before," she said, smiling. "What can I do for you, Mister Jackson? I hope you're not trying to sell me a house in this weather."

"No, I'm not," he said, wiping the rain from his face. "Can

the cellphone number is still good. She's setting up a naturo-pathic store in Oracle Plaza. Do you know it?"

"No, but I can look it up if I decide it's necessary."

Moses raised an eyebrow but kept his lips sealed.

"I have to go. They'll be concerned at the office."

"Your wife will be too," Moses said.

"My wife? What do you mean?" Jamal swallowed the large bite of pancakes into his mouth.

"You're wearing a wedding ring. I assume you're married."

"Oh. This." He slipped the band on and off his finger, trying to chase thoughts of Qaylah away. She must be worried by now; if not about him, about her money. And then there was Allie. She must be wondering where he went since he didn't return to the office. It crossed his mind for the first time that he didn't have her phone number.

"Maybe you should call her and tell her you're alright."

"I'll call her from the office," he said, rising from the couch. "Thanks for breakfast. I've got to get ready for work." Jamal straightened his clothing and stuffed the figurine into his pant pocket. He walked out of the room and ended up in the kitchen. At the front door, he scrambled to unfasten the locks and leave.

Moses caught up. "Let me help you before you damage the paint. Are you sure you can drive? Lisa's walking stick packs a punch."

"I'll be fine, Moses. Thanks for breakfast."

"You're welcome. Here, take this with you and read through it. It might help you figure out who it is that's causing the possession. And please, call my cousin. There may be times when you feel better, but the devil is a liar. It will stay inside you until it's released. Your keys!"

Jamal turned back and grabbed the keyring from Moses's hand. When he jumped into the car, he saw Moses waving from the porch. Down the street, Jamal crumpled the business card and threw it in the back seat. The figurine warmed his pocket, and he felt better.

~

HE ARRIVED at the Papyrus Hotel around noon, thought about showering, changed his mind, and dressed in record time. Next, he checked his emails. His website got an update, including new profile pictures sans beard. There were no messages from the office.

He deleted all the emails his mother and sisters sent to him. Qaylah must have told them by now that he was missing. The last thing he wanted was a gang of angry Black women telling him what he should and shouldn't be doing.

Today, he needed to meet with Tim and help Allie sell her second house. The day was shaping up to be a busy one, and he was off to a late start, thanks to Lisa and her walking stick. Damn ugly woman. Moses took one for the team marrying her.

His cellphone rang. He dug it out of his pocket but didn't recognize the number. "Hello?"

"As Salaamu Alaikum, Jamal. Please don't hang up." *Shit.*

"Qaylah, I don't have time to talk. I'm getting ready to drive to the office." He listened to her take a series of deep breaths before she spoke.

"I don't know if I'm more hurt that you abandoned us in the middle of the night and haven't come home in over a day, or because you're talking to me like I'm a friend who phoned you in the middle of your busy workday."

"I am in the middle of a busy workday."

"Where have you been? Answer me!" A jumble of static from Qaylah's end of the phone hit Jamal in the ear.

"Don't raise your voice. I'm your husband, not your child.

I'm willing to have a reasonable conversation later if you calm down."

"Calm down? Jamal, where is my money? You had no right to touch it."

"It's in a safe place," he said, sliding his feet into his loafers.

"Where is that, your bank account?"

"No. A bank asks too many questions when you deposit this kind of cash. It's somewhere safe."

"What does that mean, Jamal? Somewhere safe? Tell me in explicit terms what you've done with it, right now or—"

"Or what? You'll call the police?"

"I'm not calling the police."

"Oh, I get it. You're going to tell Brian to come over and take care of me for you, right? You want your old lover to get the new one in check."

"Why are you talking like this to me? Haven't I been a good wife to you?"

"Not good enough." Jamal hung up the phone and jammed it into his pocket. He palmed the figurine and squeezed it until the cut on his finger opened up and bled. When a voice suggested he make Qaylah go away forever, he agreed.

CHAPTER TWENTY-FIVE

JAMAL DROVE the Escalade into the parking lot and pulled into the last spot in front of Ashraf Realty, next to Renee's Acura. If it was still there later, he was going to key it. He looked for Allie's Honda but didn't see it.

It was difficult to focus through the clouded areas in his eyes, but he was certain her car was not in the lot. She must have gone to show the second house. He put on a pair of sunglasses to hide the thickening layers of white matter growing over his eyes and climbed out of the SUV, messenger bag in tow.

"Good afternoon, Jamal. You missed the meeting." Hannah perched behind the reception desk, typing away on her desktop without turning to face him. Jamal remembered when she used to treat him like an asset to the company. Now, he couldn't get her to treat him like he was human.

"Was Allie at the meeting?"

"How should I know? I'm much too busy making coffee for the perpetually empty pot in the break room and womaning the phones. I don't have time to keep up with realtors, just like I'm sure you don't have time to stand here talking to me. Good day."

I've got time to bury this pen in your skull. The thought

came out of nowhere. It excited him.

If Hannah could hear his inner monologue, what would she do? He rubbed the clay figure in short, vigorous strokes, hiding his movements behind his messenger bag.

"Okay. If you see her, tell her I need to talk to her," he said.

"Uh huh," she replied, turning back to her typing.

What a self-righteous whore. Jamal stood there staring at the side of her head a beat too long and Hannah's deft fingers halted on top of the keys.

"Do you need anything else, Jamal?"

"Nope." He beat his knuckles on the counter. She jumped.

RENEE POURED coffee into a mug as Jamal entered the break room unnoticed. He watched her pour cream and sugar into one mug, then fill another one and place them on a nearby table. She sat down and shuffled her tarot cards.

"Why do you wait on Chauncey hand and foot? Do y'all have a thing going on?"

"Jamal, you scared the daylights out of me. And no, we do not have a thing going on. Chauncey is gay."

A smile spread across Jamal's face. "That's why he's so interested in my looks."

"Don't flatter yourself. He thinks you're a charity case."

"Whatever. I don't care about Chauncey either." Jamal poured coffee into his mug and put back the empty pot.

"Aren't you going to make some more?"

"Nope."

Renee narrowed her eyes. "I knew it was you."

"You don't know shit, Renee."

"I know your ass is coming unhinged. And you know what else?"

"What?"

"I'm loving every minute."

"I'll bet you are. That's what ghetto girls are like. They feel up when you're down and revel in other people's obstacles."

"Obstacles? Honey, your life's falling apart. Your wife came in here earlier looking for you."

"Stop lying," he said.

"Why would I lie? You know, I thought you hated Black women, but the truth is you hate any woman who won't trip over herself for you. You like a weak woman, Jamal. Like Allie."

Jamal tilted his head and watched Renee shuffle her cards. "Well, I'll be damned. It's making sense now. You're the one, aren't you?"

Renee eyed him with suspicion. "What are you talking about?"

"I'm onto you, Renee. It's plain as day that you're the one doing this shit to me." He swiped her cards onto the floor, except for one.

"Motherfucker, what did you do that for?" She held up her hands, then looked at the card on the table and smiled. "Here I was, wondering how things were going for you, and it's all written right here in the cards." Renee picked it up and showed it to him. "Damn, Jamal. It sucks to be you."

Jamal shrugged. He knew shit-all about tarot. "Fuck off you wannabe." He left the break room and went to his office. The messenger bag landed on the sofa as he walked to the window. Allie's car was there. She must have slipped in while he was wasting time on Renee. He went to her office and knocked on the door.

"Come in."

Jamal opened the door and started beaming at the sight of her. She wore a black denim dress that showed off her curves.

"Oh, it's you. Have you seen Tim?"

"Tim can wait," Jamal said, closing the door. "I'm sorry that I didn't come back to the office yesterday, babe. Something came up." He moved to kiss her cheek and Allie glided away from him. Jamal laughed. "Hey, baby, what was that for? You're in a silly mood." He wrapped his arms around her waist, and she pried his hands off her.

"Knock it off, Jamal, your finger is bleeding. I have a client on the way to purchase a home. I'd like to appear professional when they arrive."

Jamal wrapped it in a tissue and fished around in his pocket for a bandage. The scruff on his chin started itching. He'd have to track down the barber at the hotel again. "Miss Lombardi?"

"No. Someone else. God, what is that smell?" Allie sprayed air freshener.

"Get out of here. You sold the other house, didn't you?"

"She sure as hell did. Allie knocked it out of the ballpark." Tim stood behind them in the doorway with a bottle of sparkling grape juice wrapped in cellophane in one arm and a bouquet of roses in the other. "Here you go, Allie. Your clients are going to flip out when you give this to them, along with the keys."

Tim brought the items into Allie's office and laid them on her small desk. "I'm proud of you, sweetheart." He grabbed her around the waist and drew her into a full-blown kiss. They broke apart, and Tim patted her on the backside.

"Thanks, baby. That means the world to me."

"Baby? Sweetheart? Allie, what the fuck is going on? Why are you kissing him?" Jamal reached into his pocket and squeezed his hand around the broken clay figure until it punctured his palm. The pain kept him from driving the bottle into Tim's brain.

Did this bitch take his money and start a fling with Tim?

"I know it's in poor taste to have office flings, but Allie and

I have a connection," Tim said. "I didn't care for her at first, but we hit it off last night after we sold The Big House."

Jamal swallowed to keep from vomiting. He ripped the sunglasses off his face and stared them down. "You what?"

"We did it, Jamal," Tim said. "We sold the condo, and we got forty thousand over the asking price. What's wrong with your eyes?" Tim stopped bouncing on his heels and peered at him. "No offense, but you look like shit today. And speaking of shit, it's kind of funky in here Allie. Light some candles or something."

Allie did as she was told, plugging in an aromatherapy mini crock. Tim had some nerve questioning Jamal's appearance. He hadn't even bothered to dress up today. His clothes looked like something to wear to a basketball game.

"Who was the buyer? One of your relatives or their friend from Singapore?"

"Actually, I found the clients," Allie said. "It was—Sarah and Asad, you're right on time. Please come inside and have a seat." Allie walked between Tim and Jamal to greet the al-Fihri family.

Jamal stood in the couple's way as they entered the room.

"Excuse us," Asad said to Jamal. He smiled and did a double take. "Jamal? Is that you? It is you; I can't believe I didn't recognize you. Why'd you shave your beard, brother?"

"That's not our business, honey," Sarah said, pulling her husband away from Jamal. She whispered something to Asad, and Jamal donned his sunglasses.

"Jamal, can we talk later? Tim is assisting me with the contracts for the house," Allie said.

"You guys went behind my back to buy a house with someone else? Some friends you are."

"Jamal," Asad began, "We're sorry—"

"You didn't return our calls when we saw the listing," Sarah said. "Allie got us into the house and showed us around as soon as we connected."

"How convenient," Jamal said. "You're all a bunch of assholes."

"Hey," Asad said, stepping forward.

"Jamal, get out," Allie said, using a tone unfamiliar to him.

He clenched his jaw and slammed the door on his way to his office. For the next hour, Jamal paced in front of his desk, wondering what was happening.

A group of Muslim men walked past his window on their way to the law firm. Fifteen minutes later, they returned, traveling in the opposite direction. The afternoon prayer had finished, and shadows spread across the office. He'd been sitting for at least an hour at his desk, clutching the figurine between his fingers. A nagging pain persisted in his finger and palm, stealing attention away from his troubles.

Jamal opened his left hand and inspected it. He reached into his desk for a paperclip and unbent it. The thin metal tool dug deep into a crack in his calloused palm. He fiddled with it, finally prying loose fragments of clay from it. The hand begged to be tended to, but he didn't care about that right now.

Jamal was a fool. In his naiveté, he'd slept with Allie on his desk and declared his undying love for her before completing the act. This wasn't how it was done. A sense of shame burned in him, but stubbornness kept him from listening to his inner sense of morality. *She's mine now. That's how it works.*

He sat upright, grasping at a fleeting thought before he lost it. Of course, it wasn't Allie's fault that this was happening. It was Tim's. That sneak was one step behind Jamal, competing for the top spot. This was no different.

Tim wanted everything Jamal had. Jamal was going to put an end to the competition and win Allie's devotion if it killed him.

CHAPTER TWENTY-SIX

"Do you know your girlfriend's ring size?" The clerk behind the counter smiled at Jamal as he perused the engagement counter. She was about Allie's build but nowhere near as special. When she leaned towards him, he smelled rotten eggs.

"I don't know. I didn't want to spoil the surprise by asking her," he said, stealing fresh air away from the clerk but still smelling it. He wondered when she'd last showered, because she was overdue.

"I understand. Not to worry. If you bring her into the store with the ring and a copy of your receipt after you propose, we can have it sized for her."

"That's good to know," he said. "There are so many."

"Would she like a birthstone? What type of jewelry does she wear?"

"Ornate pieces. They look old, like antiques," he said. "Something black, paired with silver. She's mysterious and wild. I'd describe her style as whimsical, but sexy."

"Like this?" The clerk took out her phone and showed him jewelry from a website.

"Yes, that's her style."

"Thought so," the clerk said. "She sounds a little witchy to me."

"What the hell is that supposed to mean? She's not a witch. Find me what I fucking came here to buy and keep your mouth shut."

The smile on the clerk's face fell. She took two steps backwards.

An older woman set down her shopping bags and approached the counter. "Is there a problem, miss?"

The clerk stepped closer to the counter to address the woman, giving herself a wide berth from Jamal. "Sorry about that–"

"Why are you asking her? I'm the one having problems. All you bitches are the same." Jamal slammed his hand on the glass, smearing blood. The saleswoman jumped.

The older woman took a step towards him. "You should be ashamed of yourself. I know who you are. I've seen your signs scattered around town. Don't expect my business."

The sulfuric stench overpowered his senses. Jamal felt his body go rigid, as if something had taken it over. He removed his sunglasses and leaned towards the woman's ear. "Nobody asked for your business, you rotten cunt."

Horrified, she stepped away from him. Jamal laughed at his own devilish antics. She came back, squaring her shoulders.

"Haven't had enough?"

"*La ilaha ill Allah.*" A resounding slap whipped Jamal's head to the side. His left cheek stung where a welt had formed in the shape of her hand. "Be careful who you mess with, demon. We're not all helpless little girls." She spoke a prayer in his ear, then melted into the mall crowd.

Jamal looked after her, touching the welt on his face. Horrified at his behavior, he felt like going somewhere safe to hide. He wanted to go home.

~

FOR NOW, Jamal was thinking clearly again. He was going home to his wife. They would work things out.

Whatever the sister in the mall had done to him worked. The demon's hold was gone. He felt ashamed for harassing her, but grateful that he didn't have to pay a visit to Moses' cousin Rukhsana for an exorcism. He arrived at his house, rolled down the window and threw the figure into the drainage ditch.

He felt confident that his wife would accept his apology and go back to business as usual. Jamal would simply explain about his possession. He slipped off his sunglasses and looked in the rearview mirror. His cloudy eyes would help prove it. The car turned into the driveway and stopped just shy of hitting Brian's little car.

"This guy has a lot of fucking nerve." Jamal cut the engine and threw open the Escalade's door. Anger raged inside him, filling his chest as he marched to the front door, keys in hand. He slid the house key into the keyhole, but it wouldn't turn.

"Qaylah, this is your husband. Open the door." The window next to the door rattled as the blinds opened and a pair of brown eyes stared at Jamal. The eyes disappeared, and he heard the locking mechanism spring back and the deadbolt slide before the door opened.

"Open up, Qaylah."

"What do you want?" She drew her sweater closed, refusing to look at him.

"Salaam." Jamal closed his mouth and his jaw tightened. Dark clouds rolled in from all directions and the rain poured. "Let's talk."

"Did you bring my money?"

"That's all you care about, isn't it? The money." He turned to the driveway and pointed. Rain got into his sleeve and ran down his arm, settling in his armpit. "Did I give you permission to invite that man into my house?"

"Relax, Jamal. Brian isn't here."

"Then why is his car in my driveway?"

"He loaned it to me."

"What for?"

"Errands, groceries, whatever I need it for. Does that bother you?"

"If you want to go somewhere, you have plenty of in-laws who will pick you up and drive you around town." She was pushing it with her attitude.

"And what was I supposed to tell them about your absence? That you were working on a forty-eight-hour deal at the office with Allie?"

Jamal started at the mention of Allie's name. He hoped the sunglasses concealed his surprise. Jamal rushed towards the door, forcing Qaylah into the living room. He followed her in and closed it behind him.

"What are you talking about? Why did you mention her name?"

"Do you know you talk in your sleep? You must have mentioned her name a thousand times by now. She's pretty. Red hair suits her."

"You were spying on me?"

"I saw her on the Ashraf Realty website."

Her cracking voice mirrored her pained expression. "I thought my pregnancy turned you off." She reached up and touched her red locks. "I-I thought if I could look more like what you want, you'd stop thinking about her."

"Don't talk about Allie."

"Are you having an affair? Do you plan to marry her?"

"Don't talk about Allie, Qaylah. I forbid it."

"I have a right to know what's going on, Jamal. You stole my money—"

"I didn't steal your money." He pushed Qaylah into the corner with his finger pointing at her face. "I don't need your money."

"Stop it, Jamal. Get away from me." Seeing her hands clutch her belly infuriated him.

"What are you holding yourself for? What are you implying, Qaylah? Huh?"

"Jamal, Jamal, leave my mommy alone." Katie's small feet ran across the carpet towards them. A vision of the woman attacking him danced through his mind. Jamal backhanded the little girl hard, sending her flying across the coffee table onto the sofa. Lightning cracked, illuminating the dark interior of the house.

"What did you do?" Qaylah rushed to her daughter's aid, picking up the wailing child. "My baby, my baby, Mommy's got you."

"Qaylah—"

"Get out! Don't come back, Jamal."

"I didn't mean—"

"Out!"

He looked back and forth between the mother and child, and a prickly sensation crept up the back of his neck. If they wanted him gone, so be it. Jamal made his way to the front door and opened it.

"You'd better mail a cashier's check for the full amount to me by the end of the week, Jamal. Send it overnight express if you have to." He left, slamming the door behind him.

Jamal started the car and backed down the driveway. Halfway down the street, he slammed on the brakes. A woman stood in the middle of the road. He couldn't see her face behind the red veil, but the rope wrapped around her head made it clear who she was.

She raised her blue-black hand and pointed beyond him. Jamal turned to look. When he turned back, she was gone. He made a U-turn and drove back to the house. After picking through the debris, he found Die Frau, and left. Her warmth made him shiver.

CHAPTER TWENTY-
SEVEN

IT TOOK three hours for Tim to leave Allie's house after Jamal followed them to her townhouse. Tim spending the evening with Allie, doing whatever he wanted with her left him livid. Allie kissing Tim on the front steps before he left made him want to puke. Storm clouds rolled into the area, turning his windshield wavy with streams of rain, concealing him as the smug bastard drove away in his red Durango.

Allie's house looked old, but he didn't mind living in it while he got his real estate ventures off the ground. Then, he'd buy her a home anywhere in the city, maybe the one she grew up in if it was worth the trouble. He took a deep breath to prepare himself, then rapped on the door a few times and waited. A light went on upstairs. Moments later, her shadow appeared behind the thin panels of frosted glass at the front door.

"Who is it?"

"It's your lover," Jamal said, grinning. He kept grinning like a fool as the deafening silence lingered. "It's me, Allie. It's Jamal. Can you open the door, please?"

A chill ran down his neck from the drops of rain hitting the back of his head. At long last, Allie opened the door. She flipped the collar of her bathrobe and held it close to stave off the wind and rain. Her face looked flushed and tired.

"Jamal? What are you doing here? Who told you where I live?"

"Allie, baby, I think it's gonna be nice to enjoy your company in a warm bed instead of on top of a desk. Wouldn't you like that?" Jamal reached for her, and she backed away. "What's wrong? Did Tim upset you? I saw him forcing himself on you again. Why did you let him in?"

"You're spying on me? This is my personal life, Jamal. You can't just show up on my doorstep. Please go."

"Please go?" Jamal smiled in disbelief. "Baby, it's me. I'm here now. Tim won't bother you again." He edged closer, but she took a step backwards.

"You're the one bothering me. I'm sorry, Jamal. I don't want you here."

His smile faded, and he leaned closer. Shadows loomed, bringing out the hard lines in his face. "I fucked you all over my office and you want me to leave?"

"What happens at work stays at work." She shrugged and bit the corner of a fingernail.

His eyes darkened. "What are you trying to say? Don't I mean something to you? Is Tim a fling, too?"

She shrugged. "Are you really this naïve? Haven't you ever heard of casual sex?"

"You know I don't believe in that."

Allie's forehead wrinkled. "Since when? I've known you for a short while and you're ready to throw your life away over a couple of minutes of fake moans on your desk."

"Allie, why are you acting this way? It's Tim, isn't it? He's turning you against me."

"Forget about Tim. He has nothing to do with this. I don't think we should speak anymore, in private, or at work."

"You're kidding me, right? Allie, I took you under my wing and did so much for you. I put in extra time at the office, I gave you money. Allie, I care about you."

"No, you don't. You're confused. There's nothing between us, Jamal." He wrinkled his forehead. Something must have happened while he was away. She seemed confused.

"How can you say that to me? I'm trying my hardest to start a life with you, Allie. Give me a chance to prove myself. I swear, I'll be everything you need." He felt stupid begging, but he couldn't give her up.

"Get this through your head, Jamal. I don't want you."

He glared at her through the swirling clouds covering his eyes. Reality stared him in the face.

"Cunt. You're as toxic as everyone else at the office. I want the money back, Allie. Every dime."

"I can't do that right now."

"Why not?"

"It's not here."

"Don't play with me, Allie."

"I'll bring it to the office next week. Goodnight." Allie pushed the door and Jamal sprang towards her.

"That's not good enough." He crashed against the door with his shoulder, hitting her in the face. She stumbled backwards into the house. He stepped inside and closed the door.

"Jamal, please don't."

"Next week? Next week my ass. You want to buy Frauenhaus, don't you, Allie?"

"Frauenhaus? I don't know what that is."

"Don't lie. You've been clear about your goal from the beginning. You want to buy the house and rebuild it. I know your family lost it after Alexandra murdered April. Let me guess. April was your mom and Curtis was your dad. I bet you're not even full white, are you? You're a half-breed, aren't you?"

"I don't know anybody named Alexandra, and those aren't my parents. I think you should seek therapy, Jamal. You're losing it."

"If you want to deny it, be my guest. I just want my money and I'll be gone."

"I told you. I don't have it."

"Where is it?"

"I gave it to Tim. He's investing it for me."

Jamal froze. "You fucked him and gave him my money? I'm not sure who's the bigger whore, you, or Tim."

"Please, Jamal, leave."

He stepped closer. "You stole from me."

"You told me to keep it."

"Women. A man works hard for you, and what do you do? Give it to the first dick that swings your way."

"Get out."

"No. I don't care where you get the money from. Call Tim if you need to."

"If you don't stop harassing me, I'm going to file a complaint with Ashraf when he returns. There are others in the office who will corroborate my story."

"Like who?"

"Renee, Hannah, Tim…"

His finger throbbed. "This is a life-or-death situation, Allie."

"Don't be dramatic, Jamal."

"You can give me the money, right here and now, or you can give me your life." He moved towards her, backing her into a corner.

"Stay away from me, Jamal. No! Stay away."

He grabbed her wrists and tossed her onto the sofa. He

sneered when she closed her splayed bathrobe, covering her legs. Stupid bitch. What was the point of being modest now?

Jamal reached into his pocket to grab his phone. He'd call Tim and have him swing by with his money. The clay figurine found his fingers first, and a shock wave of heat radiated throughout his body, awakening an invisible force inside him. His eyes emitted a deep red glow.

Allie gasped. "Oh my God, what's wrong with your eyes?" She held up her hands, motioning him to stay away from her. "We can work this out. I need a couple of day—"

Jamal was on her with his full weight. They toppled to the floor, and he straddled her, wrapping both hands around her throat. He watched her face turn crimson, then purplish red. Allie's legs thrashed underneath him, kicking like a swimmer breaking the surface. He refused to stop, despite her nails digging into the meat of his hands. She went still. Jamal kept squeezing until he felt the sides of her neck bones pop.

He rose from the floor and gazed at her corpse. His bloody finger traced the blue lightning branches of veins trailing up and down her legs. He yanked the bathrobe open.

Jamal unfastened his belt and undid his pants. His eyes blazed as he lowered himself between her thighs. If he was going to hell, he wanted to make sure he earned it.

WHEN JAMAL AWOKE, he lay naked in the fetal position on the floor. His stiff frame stretched out to its full height, and the joints in his arms and legs responded with a series of cracks and pops. It had been a long time since he'd slept on the floor. The last time had been at a brother's retreat at the masjid.

He searched for a light switch, howling when his leg hit the sharp corner of the coffee table. The pain lifted the fog. He remembered everything and released the contents of his stomach onto the floor.

Jamal dropped to the floor and crawled, feeling his way around the furniture, landing in puddles of cold, wet mess along the way. He'd clean it up once he turned on the damned lights. At last, he found the switch and flicked on the lights.

The caked blood on the walls and ceiling made him sick again. Entrails traipsed the sofa, and bloody limbs sat strewn about the carpet, hacked, and torn to pieces. Utter revulsion washed over him.

I'm gonna fry for this. If they catch me.

For a fleeting moment, he thought about Qaylah and Katie, and his unborn child. There was nothing he could do for them now. It was time to fend for himself.

Jamal searched every inch of the living room for his clothes but couldn't find them. Where were they? Think.

He clenched and unclenched his fists, searching from room to room. He paused in the basement, resting his hands on his hips, careful not to step in the smeared trail of blood leading to the washer.

The blackish red gore on the washing machine was something out of a horror movie. His DNA was everywhere. So was Allie's blood. He saw his clothing rotating in the dryer, the khaki pants with visible, permanent stains of blood. He put them on anyway. No one would see it if he sprinted to the Cadillac and changed into something else.

Jamal reached into his pocket and panicked. His good luck charm wasn't there. He tore up the basement stairs to the main level, searching for her. He tossed pillows, overturned the cushions, and checked underneath the sofa. She wasn't anywhere.

He searched the cabinets in the kitchen. The sink. The freezer. The fridge. The figurine wasn't there, but he did find several containers of pork blood with vinegar. "Allie, you vindictive little bitch. You really did hate that dog." Resigned to leave without his talisman he left the kitchen and picked up his shoes at the front door.

The clay figurine fell out of his left shoe. Jamal breathed a sigh of relief and pressed his lips against the warm pottery. "Forgive me. I shouldn't be so careless." He dropped it into his pocket and left the house.

Slipping into his Cadillac, he yanked the suit bag from the garment hook on the back seat. It took a good eight minutes to change, save for the suit jacket. Now wasn't the time to be formal. He needed to get the hell out of here.

A red Durango passed him on the street. With a little luck, Tim didn't notice him. Either way, it was time for Jamal to kiss Rosewood Hollow goodbye. He watched the vehicle turn into Allie's driveway and he stepped on the gas.

Bon voyage, Tim. I'll send you a postcard from Morocco.

CHAPTER TWENTY-
EIGHT

JAMAL TOSSED his bloody clothing into a dumpster behind a convenience store and instantly felt better. Washing off the stench of Allie's bodily fluids would have felt nice too, but beggars can't be choosers.

All was right with the world, except a couple of things. He needed to get the money from under the willow tree and figure out how to access it from another country. And he needed a first aid kit. The cut on his finger had reopened.

An alarming amount of blood flowed from the wound. Jamal bought a package of gauze inside the convenience store and taped a large swathe over the bleeding appendage. He wondered if it would get worse. Moses warned him it wouldn't be over until he sought help.

What was going to happen? How long did a curse last? If the person died, did their demise release it from the soul? Did he still believe in souls?

There was one person who he was certain would know the answer. Jamal drove out of the parking lot towards the highway. A tree fell across the road, causing him to swerve. He went around it, driving over some of the thick branches and continued on his way.

Darting in and out of traffic, he was of two opinions. A

part of him screamed, *Don't go*, while the other begged to be saved from the mess he'd gotten himself into. With as much strength as he could muster, he overcame the foreign, evil inside him and kept going.

The figure burned against his thigh in retaliation to his rebellion. He got off in the west end and drove to a lower middle-class neighborhood. The polite thing to do was call, but he didn't have time for that. He rang the doorbell and waited.

The porch light came on and a tall Black man opened the door. "Jamal? Wow, As Salaamu Alaikum, brother. I can't believe you're here. Come in." Reggie Jones-Ali squeezed him in a tight bear hug like he was afraid Jamal would disappear if he let go. Although Jamal returned it with far less enthusiasm, it felt good.

"Salaam, Reggie. How's it going?"

"I'm good, man. Come inside. I'll introduce you to my family." Reggie held open the door for him, but Jamal didn't want to go in there. He'd had enough of women and children.

"Sorry, Reggie, I can't right now. I have something important to talk to you about, and it's a sensitive subject." The smile faded from Reggie's lips, and he stepped outside onto the stoop.

"Lay it on me, Jamal. What's up?"

"I think someone is using black magic against me. I need your help."

~

"You write books about possession, and you can't help me? Is this your idea of a joke?" Assured that he wouldn't have to meet Reggie's family, they sat at a small table in Reggie's kitchen out of the rain. The storm had gotten worse.

Reggie hung his head over a steaming mug of tea. "Jamal, if you knew how many times people approached me to perform exorcisms, you'd understand where I'm coming from. People think they have demons inside them because someone has slighted them, or life isn't going as planned. What I can do is sit with you over the course of a couple of weeks and make an assessment. By then, you'll realize that a good therapist is all you need."

"I'm not crazy, Reggie. I'm cursed. Do you think it's normal to wear sunglasses at night? Look at my eyes." Jamal tore the sunglasses from his face and stared at him.

"What am I supposed to see, Jamal? The last time I checked, dark brown eyes didn't indicate possession."

"They're not dark brown, Reggie. I mean, they are when things are normal, but right now, they're..."

Jamal's voice trailed off as he saw his reflection in the stainless-steel toaster on the counter. He stared back at himself through his dark brown eyes.

"Sorry, Jamal. Take this number. Dr. Castleman is a good therapist. She specializes in multi-faith mental wellness."

JAMAL WANTED to phone Qaylah and tell her how stupid Reggie was, but he fought off the temptation. Reggie didn't know shit. Driving there was a waste of precious time and gasoline.

He tossed the therapist's business card out the window and rooted around in the back seat for Rukhsana Davis's. He found it and punched the number one-handed into the phone's GPS application while the storm raged around him.

Oracle Plaza housed a slew of health food stores of different varieties. He found it peculiar. Why operate next to the competition? Upon further inspection, he realized they had organized themselves according to religious affiliation.

A familiar face stood outside a health food store called Shifa'a, adjusting his cufflinks. Moses Reneau. Jamal watched him pull the door open and enter the store. He climbed out of the car and followed. The closer he got to the establishment, the more the figurine burned the top of his thigh. She didn't like it here.

A black car pulled up to the curb and deposited a brown-skinned woman in a blue hijab onto the sidewalk. She strode into Shifa'a and started talking to Moses. She laughed at something he said, then turned her attention to a stunningly tall woman wearing a turban-style hijab.

The jagged statue burned him in protest, but Jamal pushed forward towards Moses. He fought against the evil growing inside him, clawing his way through the store. The smattering of employees and the young woman turned to look at him.

"Moses, you were right all along. I'm in trouble," Jamal said. He wiped sweat from his brow as he approached his friend. "I meant to come earlier, but she wouldn't let me. She kept pulling me in, deeper and deeper. I don't know what to do, man. I did some bad things." He broke down, burying his face in his hands.

"Hey, man, it's alright." An enormous hand crushed his shoulder. "But I'm Marlon, not Moses. You're mixing me up with my little brother."

Jamal raised his head in confusion and sniffed. "You look so much alike." The tears flowed; he gave up trying to hide them. "I don't know what to do."

"Can I help you?" The elegant woman in the turban approached Jamal. She studied him for a moment, then let out a gentle sigh.

"As Salaamu Alaikum," Jamal said. "Are you Rukhsana? Moses told me to come and see you."

"Wa Alaikum As Salaam. What's your name? And why did he send you to me?"

"My name is Jamal Jackson and I need an exorcism." A glass bottle exploded near Rukhsana.

CHAPTER TWENTY-
NINE

"I'M ALRIGHT, it's a little glass. Marlon, please clean this up. Come with me, Mister Jackson." Employees scrambled. Jamal allowed Rukhsana to lead him by the hand into a room in the back of the store. Rukhsana guided him onto the table and threw a disposable sheet over his body. "Lay your head on the pillow and try to relax."

Jamal sank into the cushioned examination table and took in the quiet woman. She smelled like cocoa butter with a hint of lavender and frankincense. After a series of questions, Rukhsana agreed to administer ruqya on him to heal his body and expel whatever entity she might encounter. The Zamzam water she poured on his wounded hand burned like the devil.

"This cut is bleeding as if you sliced it to the bone, but it's not deep. It's like a paper cut. Shaytaan enters the body in various ways." Rukhsana looked into his eyes. "He's got a real hold on you." Someone on the other side of the door knocked in a sharp, hurried cadence. "Excuse me, Jamal." She pushed up from her stool and left the room.

While he waited for her, he read Rukhsana's RN credentials on the wall. It made him feel better knowing he was in the hands of a professional. Piss on Reggie and his guru antics.

The sound of hushed voices outside the door snapped

Jamal back to attention. The hoarse one was distinct and male, no doubt belonging to Moses' brother, Marlon. He wondered what was up.

Jamal swung his legs over the edge of the table and pulled out his phone. Hundreds of notifications and alerts flashed on the screen. He opened the browser and, on a hunch, typed in his name.

The headlines mentioned a massive manhunt was underway for a suspect at large. A lump settled in the middle of his throat when he saw pictures of himself. There was a before and after shot, taken from his new and old real estate signs.

"JAMAL, wait a minute. Don't leave like this, brother, let me heal you." Rukhsana chased him through the store as he bolted from the exam room.

"Heal me? You don't have that kind of power, and I don't have that kind of time. I've got to go. I was stupid to come here in the first place," he said, shooting a glance at Marlon.

"The police are looking for you," Rukhsana said. "Before they come, let me help you. You need this. It's controlling you."

Jamal's brow darkened, and he stepped towards Rukhsana. "It's inside me, but I did what I had to do. That bitch deserved everything I did to her." Rukhsana backed away, and Marlon stepped between them.

"Hey, man. I think you should go. I don't want any trouble in my cousin's store."

"You won't get any. I respect your brother, so I'll leave." Jamal stepped outside into the dim parking lot and walked to his car. He opened the door after he was sure there were no law enforcement vehicles in sight and climbed inside. He had two stops to make, then he'd be long gone.

~

JAMAL TOOK THE BACK ROADS, driving with his high beams, and windshield wipers set to the highest speed. Would it ever stop raining? He parked down the street from the house on Spiegel Road. He raced on foot to the large willow tree and plunked down into the dirt.

His bare hands sunk into the muck in a brown, muddy puddle at the base. The dirt was loose. He found the plastic bag in no time. Jamal used the water from the puddle to rinse it off. Above him, he heard a creaking rope. A pair of dangling feet swung in front of him. Alexandra. On a branch to his far right, there was another pair. April.

"I don't know what you bitches want from me. I can't give you this house. Take it from someone else. I'm leaving. He washed his hands in the muddy water and walked to his awaiting Cadillac.

Jamal turned on the engine and switched off the cold air blowing in from the air conditioning. The change in temperature fogged up the windows.

He reached into his pocket for the clay figurine. He was a believer now and needed a little luck. It was gone. Jamal shut off the engine and listened to the pitter-patter of rain on the roof. This was the loneliest night of his life. He banged his injured hand on the steering wheel and cried out.

His shoulders sagged and he stuck the finger in his mouth, sucking at the pain. It was the perfect weather for snuggling under a blanket on the couch and watching a movie. Just being together. Being boring.

He picked up the freezer bag and squeezed the bricks of

cash in his hands. Jamal wondered if Qaylah would forgive him for losing a portion of her money if he returned the rest. It might be worth it to sneak by the house for a few minutes. Just to say goodbye.

His eyes studied the outside of the bag, streaked with smeared droplets of muddy water. Jamal turned on the overhead lamp and leaned in close.

"What the hell?" He tore the bag open and pulled out a band of hundred-dollar bills and stared at it. Paper play money. A tap on the window made him jump.

"Police, show me your hands." His eyes shut against the blinding beam of light reflecting off a hundred different droplets of rainwater. Jamal turned his head away from the window. When he opened his eyes, they landed on the keys in the ignition.

"Don't do it, Jamal. It doesn't have to end this way." He smiled. Of course.

"Hey, Parker. Are you the only cop this city can afford?"

"You know how it is, brother. I'm back on the grind, working overtime to cover my vacation expenses."

"I respect your game," Jamal said, throwing up his hands. "Where'd you go?"

"Morocco."

Jamal's smiling mouth opened into a full, toothy grin. "How was it?"

The door swung open, and Officer Parker pulled Jamal to the ground and put his entire weight on top of him. The sound of the cuffs clicking and tightening around his wrists was the scariest thing he'd heard all night.

"It rained the whole damn time," Officer Parker said, lifting Jamal off the pavement. "I wish you hadn't killed that poor girl, Jamal. I don't think the capital punishment protesters will bother to come out for you. Robert, put him in your car. I don't want him in mine."

"Sure thing. Alright, creep, let's go." Officer Robert Ortega put Jamal in the back of his squad car and slammed the door. Jamal watched Officer Parker climb into his patrol car until a swarm of police cars blocked his view.

Lights came on in the neighborhood one by one, like they were on a circuit. Jamal wished he could go inside one of them to get out of the rain and call his wife. Qaylah would know what to do. This was all a big misunderstanding. If she explained it, they'd let him go, and she'd be waiting with a hot bowl of burnt stew and warm towels.

Jamal stared at the house from the back seat window. He studied his recent sign, hardly recognizing himself. In a last farewell, it flew off its hooks and disappeared into the wind.

He never wanted to see this house again. This was the first property Jamal couldn't sell. He panicked when he pictured the shock on Ashraf's face when he returned to the office. 'Not Jamal,' he'd say. 'He was my best salesman.'

A flash of lightning came down, illuminating both houses and for a fleeting moment, he saw Frauenhaus, from roof to foundation, in its former glory. A crowd of women stood on the lawn. April and Tomeeka climbed down from the tree, and they all went inside the house.

"Some old houses have lots of ghosts," he said, leaning against the glass. The police car started and drove to the station.

EPILOGUE

"He likes to move around a lot." Qaylah bounced the wiggling baby on her knee to entertain him. Jamal studied his son's features through the thick plexiglass pane, wondering who he resembled more.

"He's beautiful. I wish I could hold him, but I'm not allowed to touch visitors," he said.

"I understand." She refused to look him in the eyes. The cloudy matter still swirled in his irises. Nobody looked at him for long anymore. His lawyer pretended it wasn't there, and the people behind bars didn't care. They'd just as soon pluck them from his sockets as worry about his eye color.

He'd spent a record number of days in solitary confinement for fighting since he arrived at the penitentiary. After his arrest, Jamal allowed the jinn possessing him full access to his mind and body.

The jinni found joy in wreaking havoc on the clerical staff. They didn't visit when he sat rotting in solitary. There were too many opportunities for accidents, too many corners that video surveillance couldn't see.

The jinni whispered things, stirring up terrible memories. Fuel for his nightmares. He dreamed of Allie and that night. It thanked him for providing a vessel for it to play in, reminding him as he cursed it that had he not neglected his worship, it wouldn't have gotten in at all.

It talked about how his son would never know him. How Qaylah brought the boy this one time so she could say she wasn't a monster like Jamal. It stung when the jinni told him that Reggie Jones-Ali officiated Brian and Qaylah's marriage ceremony after his girlfriend miscarried. It was Katie who convinced her father to convert.

The jinni even told him things his mother and father wouldn't. Like how they told Brian he was welcome in their home. And how they were never going to visit Jamal. They were even thinking about offering one of Jamal's sisters as a second wife for him.

After a while, he took the jinni's word for everything. He felt like he was catching up on the scenes from a television show he'd missed.

"Jamal?" Qaylah shifted the baby onto her shoulder when he settled down and yawned. He was a few months past his first birthday. She refused to tell him the baby's name at first, but he learned it from the visitor's application. "Abdullah is a nice name," he said. She didn't respond. The baby had Brian's last name. He chose not to make it an issue.

"Yes, Qaylah?"

"Do you have access to an imam here?"

"Yeah. Sometimes." Jamal glanced at the clock and pretended not to notice when she sighed in relief. It was time to go.

She glanced at him, then looked away. "I think you should visit him. You're... it's like you're a different man. Nobody changes personalities like that unless they're..."

"They're what?"

"Far from God or sick. You've got evil inside you." She stood, careful not to wake the baby. "This is the last time you'll see your son. I can't do this again. Guard, I'd like to leave, please." The guard stepped forward to escort her to the exit.

"Congratulations on your wedding. Tell Brian I said 'As Salaamu Alaikum.'"

She walked through the door without looking back.

∿

"MAIL CALL." There were two times a day when a hush descended over Cell Block D: an hour into lights out and during mail call. A sea of orange jumpsuits crowded around inmate Alan Harmon as he brought in stacks of letters, periodicals, and postcards for the chosen ones.

Jamal stole the opportunity to watch his favorite show without fighting for a place on the couch while the usual watchers hoped for letters from home or crazy girls who liked killers. Jamal didn't expect a letter from anyone.

"Yo, Jackson. Get your mail, homie. Jamal Jackson. Wake up, man." Harmon waved an envelope in the air. Who the hell had written to him?

He turned it over in his hands, not reading who it was from. For now, having it was enough. He sniffed it, separating the prison smell from the outside world. He smelled cinnamon and sage, and something earthy.

Later on, when he finished reading it, he'd hang it on the wall and memorize every word. Jamal smirked at the envious stares. In prison, mail was everything. He planned to savor every word in this letter. It was probably the only one he'd ever get.

∿

Jamal sat on the letter for three days, wondering what might be inside the envelope. Waiting was a delicious torture. He placed it underneath his mattress, increasing the agony. He found that the anticipation made him hard, and he satisfied his lowest desires several times. When he could stand it no longer, Jamal snatched the envelope and took it to the yard.

Yesterday, KPMT News Channel Six claimed it was one hundred degrees Fahrenheit in the shade. He found a spot under a willow tree to block out the harsh sun before the guards canceled yard time altogether. Jamal's hands shook with anticipation as he tore into the envelope. He put aside a stack of postcards and pictures, then opened it.

July 24, 2018

Dear Jamal,

First, I'd like to say that I'm ecstatic with how events unfolded in the past few months, thanks to you. I couldn't have planned them any better. You went above and beyond the call of duty.

Life is hard for witches, but life is even harder for Black witches. When our benefactors showed kindness to our Black ancestors, the women in my family pledged to support them the best way we knew how; after all, we've done our share of struggling since the dark days in Salem.

They taught us to worship the goddess and she brought us great prosperity. Unfortunately, when the covenant broke, our power weakened, and we lost the house. Alexandra has finally come home.

Our old neighbor, Tobias, resentful and defiant, interfered in our grand schemes to recover the property. He hated Black people owning anything better than he had.

The sisters learned that we couldn't regain the property without atonement and a proper sacrifice. The chaos that you provided went beyond our expectations. Your evil assault has pleased Die Frau.

Before you cry foul, you have to understand. We invoked the power of the black crow—to bring you bad luck. We simply wanted you to have trouble selling the house before we came up with enough money to complete the sale. You were never supposed to break apart your family, or murder anyone, but you were so enamored with evil that you willingly became its truest vessel.

My lover, who you know as Officer Tasha Macklin, held onto Buck for a few days, but he kept sneaking off. Buck knows his way home from our place, which is right around the corner. Tobias loved that dog more than life itself; in the end, he proved it. Allie did us a favor by pretending to kill that dog. She was cooler than Chauncey and Tim gave her credit for. Anyway, Buck got out again and led us to the willow tree. He's a very good boy. We appreciate the donation you left for us.

After the scandal you caused, we purchased the land for a song and used your cash towards the cost of exhuming Alexandra and April. They are now interred in the shade of their beloved willow tree.

We'll be restoring the land to its original state, planting an herb garden, and rebuilding the house. It's a great endeavor, but so far, so good.

I can't wait to prep the flower beds and plant some black tulip seeds. I got them from a Pakistani American friend. In return, I owe her a deviously delicious love potion. We've sort of adopted her into our little family. Diversity is a wonderful thing, isn't it?

This is getting long, so I'll sign off now.

Yours in spirit, Renee Alexandra (Alex) Stillwater-Rucker.

P.S. I love my corner office. Since You're in prison and Tim went crazy after finding Allie, I automatically got the second office. My cousin, Chauncey, got the big one, of course. You always

*teased me about being second best. Work smarter, not harder,
I say.*

*P.P.S., Do you know the lore about trees? Look it up in the
prison library sometime, it's quite interesting. And lest you think
ill of us, we don't advise staying in a prolonged cursed state.
Perhaps it will lift if you seek forgiveness from your deity.*

⁓

JAMAL SAT STUNNED for the remaining half hour of yard
time. Actual pain coursed through him, clenching his heart,
then settling like a stone in the pit of his stomach.

He turned over the postcard and viewed the picture of the
large house on the front, flanked by willow trees. An inset
photo showed a group of little Black girls in braids and
turquoise veils gathered around one of the trunks. Jamal wiped
the sweat from his brow as he studied their faces.

Left of center, a little dark skinned Black girl wearing a red
veil smiled at the camera. The taller girl next to her wore a
turquoise veil. Fiery locs hung from it. He read the hand-
written names at the bottom. *Alex, age seven, and Tasha Macklin, age fourteen.*

Open weeping in this place meant death. Jamal lay his head
against the willow tree, releasing a swell of emotions by
pounding his fist into the trunk. A series of vibrations traveled
through him, and he fell into a stunned silence. His fingers
opened, and he rested his hand against the tree's trunk. In his
palm, he felt a rhythmic beat.

"Astaghfirullah. Oh Allah, forgive me," he said, breaking
down into a hard sob. He didn't care who saw. It was time to
call upon his Lord. The scales fell from his eyes. He watched as
the scar tissue and pain in his hand faded. The guards blew
their whistles in the yard, calling him home.

Nakia Cook was born in Atlanta, the other Atlanta, in Cass County, Texas. People think she made it up, but if you squint at the map hard enough, you'll find it. Most of her characters live in Rosewood Hollow, Virginia, which she did make up. It takes a lot to spook her, but when it happens, it's usually a small kid standing in the shadows in the middle of the night.

Sign up for Nakia's newsletter for title and cover reveals and information about new releases once in a while.

www.nakiacook.com